"We are still married."

"Why do you keep on saying that?" Frankie demanded in sudden flaring repudiation. "It's just not true!"

"Five years ago you made only a brief initial statement to your solicitor, who advised you to consult another solicitor, one more experienced in the matrimonial field. No further action was taken," Santino completed dryly.

Frankie trembled. There was something horribly convincing about Santino's growing impatience with her. "If there's been some stupid oversight, I'm sorry, and I promise that I'll take care of it as soon as I go home again—"

"Five years ago I would have agreed to an annulment." Santino surveyed her tense face with cool, narrowed eyes. "Indeed, then I considered it my duty to set you free. But that is not a duty that I recognize now. To be crude, Francesca...I now want the wife I paid for."

D0822283

LYNNE GRAHAM was born in Northern Ireland and has been a keen romance reader since her teens. She is very happily married, with an understanding husband who has learned to cook since she started to write! Her five children, four of whom are adopted, keep her on her toes. She has a very large wolfhound, who knocks over everything with her tail, and an even more adored crossbreed, who rules everybody. When time allows, Lynne is a keen gardener and loves experimenting with Italian cookery.

Books by Lynne Graham

HARLEQUIN PRESENTS

LYNNE GRAHAM

The Reluctant Husband

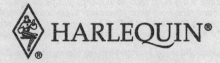

TORONTO • NEW YORK • LONDON
AMSTERDAM • PARIS • SYDNEY • HAMBURG
STOCKHOLM • ATHENS • TOKYO • MILAN • MADRID
PRAGUE • WARSAW • BUDAPEST • AUCKLAND

ISBN 0-373-11971-2

THE RELUCTANT HUSBAND

First North American Publication 1998.

CHAPTER ONE

MATT FINLAY scanned Frankie's shocked face and gave her a bracing smile. 'I happen to think that Sardinia could be a very therapeutic trip for you. You could confront your memories of the love of your life and get it all out of your system—'

'Santino was hardly the love of my life!' Frankie countered between gritted teeth, her whole body tense as a drawn bow.

Matt frowned with pretended concentration. 'I seem to recall that every time you saw the bloke you went weak at the knees and your little teenybopper heart turned cartwheels!'

The evils of alcohol on a loose tongue at the office party, Frankie reflected painfully. One of those times when she had tried a little too hard to be accepted as one of the boys. She should have known Matt would throw that confession back in her face one day when it suited him. 'I spent five of the worst years of my life in Sardinia. You can't blame me for not wanting to go back.'

'You could be off the island again within forty-eight hours and go on to Italy. It wouldn't need to interfere with your holiday plans. Who else is there? Dan's still in France and Marty's wife is due to give birth any day now...'

Frankie wanted to appeal to him again but her sense of fairness would not allow it. Their travel agency, of which she herself owned a sizeable share, specialised in self-catering accommodation abroad, and business had not been that good in recent months. They had lost more than the usual number of properties to competitors. Times were tough in the holiday market.

She squared her shoulders, a tall young woman with the sleek, graceful lines of a thoroughbred, dressed in a sharply tailored black trouser suit, quite deliberately chosen to play down her femininity. She had a fine bone structure, with clear green eyes fringed by ebony lashes and set below equally dark brows. Her burnished hair, a fiery combination of red, copper and gold, was worn in a French plait, embellished by a velvet bow clip. That clip was her one concession to being female.

'And you're a native,' Matt mused with satisfaction. 'That has to be to our advantage.'

'I'm British,' Frankie reminded him flatly.

'Six villas on the Costa Smeralda. You check them out, sign up the owner, go on to Italy and we're in business. And who knows...? By the time you come home from your holiday, you might even be in the mood to celebrate with me over a romantic dinner for two,' Matt suggested with a slow, suggestive smile.

Discomfited by that look, Frankie tensed and coloured. They were friends, but Matt had recently strained their friendship by trying to persuade her into a more intimate relationship. She had already told him as tactfully as she could that she wasn't interested and his persistence was making her increasingly uncomfortable. After all, not only did they work together, they also had to live under the same roof.

'No chance,' she told him with a rather forced grin as she walked to the door.

'Sometimes I hate your brother,' Frankie informed the smiling blonde manning the counter outside.

Leigh just laughed. 'Sardinia?'

'You *knew*?' Frankie felt betrayed and knew she was being oversensitive. Neither of her friends could be expected to understand how threatened she felt by the thought of setting foot on the island again. After all, she hadn't told either of them the full truth of what had happened to her there. 'Why didn't you warn me?'

'Matt thought you'd take it better coming from him, and you'll only arrive for your holiday in Italy sooner,' Leigh pointed out cheerfully as she turned away to answer the phone.

Frankie's long legs made short work of the stairs up to the spacious two-bedroom apartment which she had shared alone with Matt since Leigh had got married. She had moved in with the Finlay siblings three years earlier. Using the proceeds of an insurance policy which had matured when she was eighteen, she had bought into the business. The agency was on the ground floor of the same building. Since Frankie now spent most of her time travelling, spot-checking the standards of current properties and negotiating for new ones, she found the location very convenient.

Or at least she had until Matt had begun acting up, she conceded ruefully. His recent innuendos and familiarities hadn't gone unnoticed by their employees either. The office tongues were already wagging and gossip upset Frankie. A long time ago she had learnt to her cost that careless talk could wreck lives. It had, after all, very nearly destroyed hers once. She shook off that memory with an inner shudder. Did Matt see her as some sort of a challenge? She wasn't even his type. Why were men so infuriatingly contrary? The sooner Matt went back to chasing his trademark tiny blondes, the happier she would be.

She rang her mother's home. The maid answered and put her through.

'Mum? I'm going away earlier than expected,' she said apologetically.

'Frankie...don't you think you're getting rather too long in the tooth to be calling me Mum?' Della snapped in petulant reproof. 'It makes me feel as if I should be collecting my pension!'

'Sorry.' Frankie bit her lip uneasily, a shard of pain that was all too familiar piercing her as Della brushed off the news of her coming absence without comment or indeed any perceptible interest. 'I have to go to—'

'I have an appointment with my manicurist in an hour,' Della interrupted impatiently. 'I'll call you some time next month.'

Frankie replaced the receiver, her hand not quite steady. No matter how many times it happened, it still hurt. All the old excuses came flooding back. Her mother had a very busy social life. She was not a demonstrative person. Those years of separation when Frankie had been in Sardinia had damaged their relationship. But at the back of her mind always lurked the insecure fear that her mother would really not have noticed if her daughter had *never* come home again. And then she felt deeply ashamed of herself for even thinking such a thing.

Frankie's eyes flashed with growing exasperation. It was early evening and she was thoroughly fed up. Today she had expected to be on a ferry to Genoa, in Italy, and what was she doing instead? She was cooped up in a hideously noisy little Fiat, travelling along narrow, steep Sardinian roads that forced her to drive at a snail's pace. Why? Signor Megras, the owner of the villas, had not condescended to meet her at his properties.

She had been given the grand tour by an employee and now *she* had to travel deep into the mountainous interior of the island to negotiate with the owner at his hotel. The drive had already taken far longer than she had anticipated. Of course, she could have taken advantage of the lift she had been offered by the employee, Pietro—he of the sexually voracious dark eyes and the overly eager-to-touch hands. In remembrance, Frankie grimaced. Welcome back to Sardinia, Frankie, home of the macho male and the child-bride...

As swiftly as that designation slunk into her thoughts,

she suppressed it again. She knew what was wrong with her. It was these mountains, the same mountains that had imprisoned her for five unforgettable years. Her flesh chilled at the memories, so why should she let them out? That was the past and it was behind her. She was twenty-one now, and fully in control of her own life again.

But still the memories persisted. The culture shock of being eleven years old, one moment living a civilised life in London and the next being suddenly thrust unprepared into the midst of an almost illiterate peasant family, who didn't even want her. The horror of being told that she would never see London or her mother again. The desertion of her father within days. The loneliness, the fear, the terrifying isolation. All those feelings were still trapped inside Frankie and she knew she would never be free of them.

Her mother had been an eighteen-year-old model when she became pregnant by a handsome Sard photographer called Marco Caparelli. The resulting marriage had been stormy. Her parents had finally separated when Frankie was eight. Her father had stayed in touch but on a very irregular basis, generally showing up when he was least expected and rarely appearing when he was. Once or twice he had even contrived to talk his way back beneath the marital roof again. Frankie's desperate hope that her parents would reconcile had seemed like a real possibility to her on those occasions.

So, perhaps understandably, she had been upset when her mother met another man and finally decided that she wanted a divorce. Della's plans had outraged her estranged husband as well. There had been a terrible argument. One day, shortly after that, Marco had picked Frankie up from school. They were going on a little holiday, he had told her and no, she didn't need to go home to pack, he had laughed, displaying the small case which he'd explained contained everything that she might need for the wonderful trip he was taking her on.

'Does Mum know?' She had frowned.

And then he had let her into the even more wonderful secret. Mum and Dad were getting back together again. It might seem a big surprise to her, but while she had been at school Mum and Dad had made up. Wasn't she pleased that she wasn't going to have a stepfather after all? And wouldn't it be fantastic when Mum joined them in Sardinia at the end of the week?

Bitterly rejecting the memory of that most cruel lie of all, Frankie rounded another corkscrew bend on the tortuous road and saw the sign at the head of a tumbledown bridge. 'La Rocca', it said. At last, she thought, accelerating up the hill into the village, braking first to avoid a goat and then two pigs. Her surroundings gave her a bad case of the chills. A clutch of scrawny hens scattered as she climbed out of the car in the dusty square.

The village was so poor you could taste it, and the taste of that poverty made Frankie shiver. She was reminded of another village even more remote from civilisation. Sienta, that particular cluster of hovels had been called. Birthplace of her paternal grandfather. Sienta had been a dot on the map of another world.

The silence grated on her nerves. Where was the hotel? She hoped it was reasonable, since she was probably going to be forced to spend the night there. Twenty yards away, through an open doorway, she saw a café. Her nose wrinkled fastidiously as she peered into the dim interior. The thick-set man behind the bar stared stonily back at her.

'Could you tell me where Hotel La Rocca is?' she asked in stilted Italian.

'Francesca…?'

Gooseflesh broke out on her arms, her every muscle jerking painfully tight. That name she never used, that voice…the soft, mellow syllables as smooth and fluid as honey yet as energising for Frankie as the siren on a police car riding her bumper. There was a whirring in

her eardrums. Slowly, very slowly, her feet began to
turn, her slender body unnaturally stiff as she fought her
disorientation, refusing to accept her instantaneous recognition of that voice.

Santino Vitale fluidly uncoiled his long, lean length
from behind the table in the far corner and moved si-
lently out of the shadows. Her tongue welded to the dry
roof of her mouth. Her skin felt damp and clammy. For
a moment she seriously doubted her sanity and the evi-
dence of her own eyes. In an exquisitely cut silver-grey
suit, an off-white raincoat negligently draped across his
shoulders, Santino looked shockingly alien and exotic
against the shabby backdrop of scarred tables and grimy
walls.

'Would you like to join me for a drink?' Dark eyes
as stunningly lustrous as black jet whipped over her
stilled figure. Smoothly he captured her hand, warmth
engulfing her fingertips. 'Ah...you're cold,' Santino
sighed, shrugging off his coat to drape it slowly and
carefully round her rigid shoulders.

Frankie stood there like a wax dummy, so overpowered by his appearance, she could not react. Shattered,
she couldn't drag her gaze from him either. At six feet
four, he towered over her in spite of her own not incon-
siderable height. Devastatingly handsome, he had the
hard classic features of a dark angel and the deeply disturbing sexual charisma of a very virile male. Without
warning a tide of remembered humiliation engulfed her,
draining every scrap of colour from her cheeks. Everything that Frankie had struggled so hard to forget over
the past five years began to flood back.

'*This* is the La Rocca hotel,' Santino murmured.

'This place?' Complete bewilderment and the sense
of foolishness that uncertainty always brought made
Frankie sound shrill.

'And you are here to meet a Signor Megras?'

'How do you know that?' Frankie demanded shakily.

'Just how do you know that? And what are *you* doing here?'

'Why don't you sit down?'

'Sit down?' she echoed, dazed green eyes scanning him as if he might disappear in a puff of smoke at any moment.

'Why not? I see no Signor Megras.' Santino spun out a chair in silent invitation. The proprietor hurried over to polish the ashtray and then retreated again. 'Won't you join me?'

A faint shaft of sunlight pierced the gloom, highlighting the tattered posters on the wall and the worn stone floor. Every natural instinct spurred Frankie to flight. She reached the door again without the awareness that she had even moved her feet.

'Are you afraid of me now?'

Frankie stopped dead, nervous tension screaming through her rigidity as a rush of daunting confusion gripped her. For an instant she felt like an adolescent again, the teenager who had once slavishly obeyed Santino's every instruction. She had been so terrified of losing his friendship, she would have done anything he told her to do. But no, Santino had not taught her to be afraid of him...she had had to learn for herself to be afraid of the frighteningly strong feelings he aroused inside her.

Was it *his* fault that she hated him now? She didn't want to think about whether or not she was being fair. Instead she found herself turning to look back at him again, somehow answering a need within herself that she could not withstand. And inexplicably it was like emerging from the dark into the light, heat and energy warming her, quelling that sudden spurt of fear and making her bite back her bitterness. Slowly, stiffly, she walked back and sank into the seat.

'What are you doing here?' she asked baldly.

'Signor Megras won't be coming. The villas belong to me.'

As the silence pulsed, Frankie stared back at him incredulously. 'I don't believe you.'

A slashing smile curved Santino's wide, sensual mouth. 'It is the truth. I brought you up here. I wanted to see you again.'

'Why?' Her head was spinning.

'You are my wife. It may be a long time since I have chosen to remind you of that fact, but you are *still* my wife,' Santino imparted with measured emphasis.

A jerky laugh of disbelief fell from Frankie's dry lips. 'Our marriage was annulled as soon as I went back to the UK,' she scorned, tilting her chin. 'Didn't you get the papers?'

Santino merely smiled again. 'Did you?'

Her brow furrowed, her mouth tightening. 'Mum has them. Since I was under-age, she dealt with the formalities—'

'Is that what you were told?'

'Look, I *know* that that ceremony was set aside as null and void!'

'You've been had,' Santino drawled with lazy amusement.

An angry flush washed over her cheeks. His persistence infuriated her. 'When I get home, I'll ensure that you're sent confirmation of the fact. I can assure you that we are no longer married.'

'But then we never were…in the adult sense,' Santino conceded.

Attacked without warning by a cruel Technicolor replay of her last sight of Santino, Frankie paled, her stomach giving a violent lurch. Santino with another woman, locked together in the throes of a very adult passion. A beautiful blonde, her peach-tinted nails spearing into his luxuriant black hair as he kissed her, melding every line of her curvaceous body to the lean, muscular strength of

his. Frankie had been ripped apart by that glimpse of
Santino as she herself had never seen him, and in that
same instant she had been forced to see that they had
never had a future together. In leaving, she had set them
both free.

Dark golden eyes rested intently on her. 'I deeply regret the manner of our parting. You were very distressed.'

Shattered that he should have guessed what was on
her mind, Frankie went rigid. In self-defence, she focused on the table. She couldn't think straight. Her emotions, usually so wonderfully well-disciplined, were in
wild turmoil. She could barely accept that she was actually *with* Santino again, but even that bewildering
awareness was pounded out of existence by the tremendous pain he had cruelly dredged back up out of her
subconscious. With fierce determination, she blocked
those memories out.

'Perhaps it was a mistake to mention that so soon but
I can feel it standing between us like a wall,' Santino
incised very quietly.

The assurance sent Frankie's head flying up again, a
fixed smile of derision pasted to her lips. 'And I think
you're imagining things. So I discovered that my saint
had feet of clay.' She shifted a slim shoulder dismiss-
ively. 'All part of growing up, and irrelevant after this
length of time. Now, if those villas really are yours, can
we get down to business?'

'You have indeed been away a long while.' Santino
signalled to the proprietor with a fluid gesture. 'That's
not how we do business here. We share a drink, we talk,
maybe I invite you to my home for dinner and then,
possibly after dinner, we get down to business.'

Frankie's expressive eyes flashed. 'I won't be coming
to your home for dinner, I assure you—'

'Strive to wait until you're invited,' Santino traded
gently.

Her cheeks reddened, her teeth gritting as wine arrived. 'I find this whole stupid charade juvenile!'

'As I remember it, you love the unexpected.' Santino lounged back indolently in his seat, unconcerned by her growing anger and frustration.

'I was a child then—'

'Yet at the time you kept on telling me that you were *all* woman,' Santino reminded her in a black velvet purr of wry amusement.

The worst tide of colour yet crimsoned Frankie's throat. 'So tell me,' she said sharply, absolutely desperate for a change of subject, 'are you in the tourist trade now?'

'This and that.' Hooded night-dark eyes resting on her, Santino lifted a broad shoulder in an infinitesimal shrug and a half-smile played maddeningly about his mobile mouth.

It was ridiculous that she shouldn't know what business he was in, ridiculous that she should know so very little about this male to whom she had once been married! But years ago all she had known about Santino was that the elderly village priest was his great-uncle and that during the week he worked in a bank in Cagliari, where he also had the use of an apartment.

But, whatever Santino was doing now, he appeared to be doing very well. That magnificent suit simply shrieked expensive tailoring. But then he was a Latin male, and the Latin male liked to look good and was quite capable of spending a disproportionate amount of his income on his wardrobe. Even so, Frankie wasn't used to seeing Santino in such formal attire. When he had come home to her at weekends, he had worn jeans and casual shirts. He looked so different now, like some big city business tycoon, stunningly sophisticated and smooth. The acknowledgement sharply disconcerted her.

Santino was surveying her with veiled eyes. 'I had a good reason for arranging this discreet meeting.'

'April Fool off-season?' Frankie derided brittly.

'I understand that you're on vacation and I would like to offer you the hospitality of my home,' Santino contradicted her evenly.

Frankie stared back at him wide-eyed and then a choked laugh escaped her. 'You're kidding me, right?'

Santino pressed her untouched glass of wine towards her. 'Why should I be?'

'I'm leaving for Italy immediately,' she told him, incredulous that he should advance such an invitation. 'So I'm afraid we do business now or not at all.'

'I don't give a damn about the villas,' Santino countered very drily.

'It's my job to give a damn.' Her sense of unreality was spreading by the minute. Santino here...with her. It felt so fantastically unreal. Why should Santino want to see her again after so long? Simple curiosity? Clearly he had found out where she worked in London. Was that why the villas had been offered to Finlay Travel? But how had Santino discovered where she worked?

From below her lashes she watched him as she drank, easing her parched vocal cords. He was so cool, so controlled...so *calculating*? Her spine tingled, some sixth sense spooking her. She scanned his gypsy-dark features, absorbing the stunning symmetry of each. The wide forehead, the thin, arrogant blade of a nose, the blunt high cheekbones and the chiselled curve of his sensual mouth. Her attention roved to his thick black hair, the curls ruthlessly suppressed by an expert cut, and the lustrous, very dark eyes which flared gold in emotion, and yet still a nagging sense of disorientation plagued her.

Santino both looked and *felt* like a stranger, she acknowledged dazedly, more than that even...a disturbingly intimidating stranger, who wore a cloak of natural authority and command as though he had been born to it. He was not Santino Vitale as she remembered him.

Or was it that she now saw more clearly without adoration blinding her perception? *Adoration?* Inwardly she shrank, but there was no denying that that single word most accurately described the emotions which Santino had once inspired in her.

'Francesca…'

'Nobody calls me that any more,' Frankie muttered waspishly, striving to rise above an ever-increasing sense of crawling mortification.

This encounter *was* a nightmare, she conceded, stricken. At sixteen, she had been so agonisingly, desperately in love with Santino. She had thrown herself at his head and done and said things that no woman in her right mind would want to recall once she reached the age of maturity! She must have seemed pathetic in his eyes, forever swearing undying love and resisting his every move to sidestep the intimacy which she had craved and which *he* had never wanted. It hadn't been Frankie who had locked her bedroom door at night…it had been Santino who'd locked *his*. That particular recollection made her feel seriously unwell.

'Look at me…' A lean brown forefinger skated a teasing path across her clenched knuckles. 'Please, Francesca…' he urged gently.

It was like being prodded by a hot wire. Her sensitive flesh scorched and she yanked her hand back out of reach, shaken by a sudden excruciating awareness of every skin-cell in her humming body. Oh, dear heaven, *no*, she thought as she recognised the wanton source of that overpowering physical response. In horror, she lifted her lashes to collide with glittering gold eyes. Her breath tripped in her throat. Her heart hammered wildly against her ribs.

'What do you want?' she demanded starkly.

'Three weeks out of time,' Santino admitted softly. 'I want us to spend that time together.'

'I'm not spending *any* time with you!' Frankie jerked upright, wide green eyes alight with disbelief.

Santino rose at his leisure, grim amusement curling his eloquent mouth. In a single fluid step he reached her. Lean hands confidently tugged her out from behind the table into the circle of his arms. Frankie was so taken aback she just stood there and looked up at him in open bewilderment. She could not credit that Santino would make any form of sexual advance towards her and uneasily assumed that he was trying to be fraternally reassuring.

'Relax,' Santino urged lazily, brushing a straying strand of bright hair back from her indented brow.

At that careless touch her heartbeat lurched violently, her throat tightening. Suddenly she was struggling to get air into her lungs. He angled his dark head down and she came in conflict with shimmering dark golden eyes. Another wanton frisson of raw excitement arrowed through her. Her head swam. Her knees wobbled. And then, before she could catch her breath again, Santino brought his mouth down on hers with ruthless precision, expertly parting her soft lips to let his tongue hungrily probe the moist, tender interior within.

That single kiss was the most electrifyingly erotic experience Frankie had ever had. Heat flared between her thighs, making her quiver and moan in shattered response. Instinctively she pushed into the hard heat of his abrasively masculine body. He crushed her to him with satisfying strength. Then he lifted his arrogant dark head and gazed down at her, his brilliant gaze raking over her stunned face as he slowly, calmly set her back from him again. 'All this time I wondered...now I *know*,' he stressed with husky satisfaction.

Frankie turned scarlet. Appalled green eyes fixed to him, she backed away fast. 'You know nothing about me!' she gasped, stricken.

In a tempest of angry distress, her only desire to escape from the scene of her own humiliation, Frankie stalked out into the fading daylight. There she blinked in bemusement before she raced across the square. It was empty...empty of her car!

'And now, thanks to you, my car's been stolen!' Frankie shrilled back at Santino where he now lounged with infuriating indolence in the doorway of the bar.

He straightened fluidly and strolled towards her. 'I stole it,' he informed her, seemingly becoming cooler and ever more dauntingly assured with every second that made her angrier.

'You did *what*?' Frankie enunciated with extreme difficulty.

'I am responsible for the disappearance of your car.'

The sort of blinding rage Frankie had honestly believed she had left behind in her teens swept over her. That cool, utterly self-possessed tone affected her like paraffin thrown on a bonfire. 'Well, you just bloody well get it back, then!' She launched at him, both of her hands closing into fists of fury. 'I don't know what kind of a game you think you're playing here—'

'I don't feel remotely playful,' Santino slotted in smoothly.

Frankie took a seething stride forward and grabbed him by the lapels of his jacket. 'I want my car back *now*!'

'The Caparelli Curse,' Santino remarked softly, reflectively, quite unmoved by the spitting frenzy of her fury. 'To think I thought rumour exaggerated. No longer does it surprise me that your grandfather was so desperate to marry you off.'

And that was it. At the mention of the hated nickname she had acquired in her grandfather's village Frankie shuddered, and when Santino went on to remind her that he had been virtually forced into marrying her her last shred of control went. 'You swine!' she hissed, and drew back a step the better to take a swing at him.

But Santino was faster on his feet than she had anticipated, and as he sidestepped her the heel of her shoe caught on the lining of the long raincoat still hanging from her shoulders. She lost her balance and went down with a cry of alarm, striking her head. There was pain...then darkness, then nothing as she slid into unconsciousness.

CHAPTER TWO

FRANKIE had a headache when she drifted back to wakefulness with a frown. But worse was to come. She lifted her heavy eyelids and focused not on her familiar bedroom but on a completely strange room. It was the most disorientating experience of her life.

Stone walls...*stone* walls? Massive antique furniture with more than an air of gothic splendour. Her mouth fell wide as she took in the narrow casement windows, for all the world like the windows of a castle. It was a vast room and the bed was of equally heroic proportions.

And only then did splinters of disconnected imagery return to her. She recalled a nun...a *nun*? She remembered feeling horribly sick, and being so. She remembered being told firmly that she had to stay awake when all that she wanted to do was sleep because her head ached unbearably. All the pieces were confused but one particular image, which had strayed in and out of her hazy impressions, struck her afresh with stunning effect...*Santino*!

A flicker of movement at the corner of her vision jerked her head around. A lithe, dark male figure stepped out of the shadows into the soft pool of light by the bed. Everything came back at once in a rush. Planting two hands on the mattress beneath her, Frankie reeled up into a sitting position, a tangle of multicoloured hair flying round her flushed and taut face. '*You!*' she exclaimed accusingly.

'I'll call the doctor,' Santino responded, reaching forward to tug the tapestry bell-rope hanging beside the bed.

'Don't bother!' Frankie asserted between clenched teeth, throwing back the sheet with the intention of getting up and then swaying as a sick wave of dizziness assailed her.

As she pressed her fingers to her swimming head, a pair of strong arms enclosed her and she was pushed firmly back down again on the pillows.

'Get your hands off me!' Frankie bit out, refusing to surrender to her own bodily weakness.

'Shut up,' Santino said succinctly, bending over her with a shockingly menacing expression stamped on his vibrantly handsome features. 'Bad temper put you in that bed and it might have killed you!'

Frozen by outrage, Frankie gaped at him, emerald-green eyes almost out on shocked stalks that he should *dare* to speak to her like that. 'Your crazy games put me in this bed!'

'Your injuries could have been far more serious,' Santino told her with a most offensive edge of condemnation. 'Had I not managed to break your fall, you might have suffered more than a sore head and concussion. You were unconscious for many hours!'

'It's your fault that I got hurt!'

'*My* fault?' Santino repeated incredulously. 'You took a swing at me!'

'The next time, I won't miss! Where the heck am I?' Frankie flared back furiously. 'I want to go home!'

'But you are home. You are with me,' Santino drawled in a soft tone of finality.

'You're nuts…you are absolutely stark, staring mad!' Frankie exclaimed helplessly, huge, bewildered eyes pinned to him. 'What did you do with my car?'

'As you were no longer in need of it, I had it returned to the hire firm.'

The door opened, breaking the thrumming silence. A tall, distinguished man in his fifties entered the room. 'I am Dr Orsini, Signora Vitale.' He set a medical bag on the cabinet by the bed. 'How are you feeling now that you have had some sleep?'

'I am not Signora Vitale,' Frankie said shakily, beginning to feel like somebody playing a leading role in a farce.

The doctor looked at Santino. Santino smiled, raised his lustrous dark eyes heavenward and shifted a broad shoulder in a small shrug.

'What are you looking at him like that for?' Frankie launched suspiciously. 'I am not this man's wife, Dr Orsini. In fact I have never seen him before in my life!' she concluded with impressive conviction.

The doctor studied her with narrowed eyes and a frown. Frankie looked with expectant triumph at Santino, but Santino was already lifting something off the enormous dressing table and extending it to the older man.

'What's that? What are you showing him?' Frankie demanded jerkily, falling fast into the grip of nervous paranoia.

'One of our wedding photographs, *cara mia*.' Santino shot her rigid stillness a gleaming glance from beneath luxuriant black lashes and tossed the silver-framed photo onto the bed for her perusal.

Without reaching for it—indeed her fingers chose to clutch defensively into the bedspread instead—Frankie stared down fulminatingly at that photograph. Her throat closed over, the strangest lump forming round her vocal cords. There she was in all her old-fashioned wedding finery, sweet sixteen and so sickeningly infatuated that she glowed like a torch for all to see, her face turned up to Santino's adoringly. Shame she hadn't had the wit to notice that Santino's smile had more than a suggestion of stoically gritted teeth about it than a similiar romantic fervour!

Quite irrationally, her eyes smarted with tears. Suddenly she appreciated that whether it was fair or not she really *did* hate Santino! He hadn't had to go through with the wedding. When he had realised the gravity of the situation they were in, surely he could have smuggled her back out of the village again and sent her home to her mother in London? She refused to believe that he could not have found some other way out of their predicament, rather than simply knuckling down to her grandfather's outrageous demand that he marry her!

The doctor was opening his bag when she lifted her head again. Throwing Santino an embittered glance, Frankie cleared her throat. 'This man may once have been my husband but he is not any more. In fact—'

'*Cara...*' Santino chided in a hideously indulgent tone.

'He stole my car!' Frankie completed fiercely.

Carefully not looking at her, Dr Orsini said something in a low, concerned undertone to Santino. Santino sighed, contriving to appear more long-suffering than ever.

'Did you hear what I said?' Frankie's voice shook.

The older man was too busy shaking his head in wonderment.

Santino strolled to the foot of the bed. 'Francesca...' he murmured. 'I know I am not your favourite person right now, but these wild stories are beginning to sound a little weird.'

Her jaw dropped. She flushed scarlet and experienced such a spasm of frustrated fury that she was dimly surprised that she did not levitate off the bed. She slung Santino a blazing look that would have felled a charging rhino. It washed over him. For the very first time she recalled Santino's wicked sense of humour. His sensual mouth spread into a teeth-clenchingly forgiving smile, white teeth flashing against his sun-bronzed skin. '*Grazie, cara...*'

'You will be relieved to learn that the X-rays were completely clear,' Dr Orsini told her in a bracing voice.

He didn't believe her; the man did not *believe* a word she had said!

'X-rays...what X-rays?' she mumbled.

'You were X-rayed last night while you were still unconscious,' Santino informed her.

'*Last* night...?' she stressed in confusion.

Santino nodded in grim confirmation. 'You didn't regain consciousness until the early hours of this morning.'

'Where was I X-rayed?' she pressed.

'In the infirmary wing of the Convent of Santa Maria.'

Am I in a convent? Frankie wondered dazedly, her energy level seriously depleted by both injury and shock upon succeeding shock. In a room kept for the use of well-heeled private patients?

'Your husband was most concerned that every precaution should be exercised,' the older man explained quietly. 'Try to keep more calm, *signora*.'

'There's nothing the matter with my nerves,' Frankie muttered, but she couldn't help noticing that nobody rushed to agree with her.

Her head was aching and her brain revolving in circles. While she endured a brief examination, and even answered questions with positive meekness, on one level she was actually wondering if she was still unconscious. All this—the strange environment, the peculiar behaviour of her companions—might simply be a dream. It was a most enticing conviction. But there was something horrendously realistic about Santino's easy conversation with the doctor as he saw him to the door, apologising for keeping him out so late and wishing him a safe journey home. Her Italian was just about good enough to translate that brief dialogue.

As Santino strode back to the foot of the bed, Frankie reluctantly abandoned the idea that she was dreaming. With an unsteady hand, she reached for the glass of water by the bed and slowly sipped.

'Are you hungry?' Santino enquired calmly.

Frankie shook her head uneasily. Her stomach felt rather queasy. She snatched in a deep, quivering breath. 'I want you to tell me what's going on.'

Santino surveyed her with glittering golden eyes, his eloquent mouth taking on a sardonic curve. 'I decided that it was time to remind you that you had a husband.'

Frankie froze. 'For the last time…you are *not* my husband!'

'Our marriage was not annulled, nor was it dissolved by divorce. Therefore,' Santino spelt out levelly, 'we are still married.'

'No way!' Frankie threw back. 'The marriage was annulled!'

'Is that really your belief?' Santino subjected her to an intent appraisal that made her pale skin flush.

'It's not just a belief,' Frankie argued vehemently. 'It's what I know to be the truth!'

'And the name of the legal firm employed on the task…it was Sweetberry and Hutchins?' Santino queried.

Frankie blinked uncertainly. She had only once visited the solicitor, and that had been almost five years earlier. 'Yes, that was the name…and the very fact that you know it,' she suddenly grasped, 'means that you know very well that we haven't been married for years!'

'Does it?' Santino strolled over to the windows and gracefully swung back to face her again. 'A marriage that is annulled is set aside as though it has never been in existence. So would you agree that if our marriage *had* been annulled so long ago I would have no financial obligation towards you?'

Confused as to what he could possibly be driving at, Frankie nodded, a tiny frown puckering her brows. 'Of course.'

'Then perhaps you would care to explain why I have been supporting you ever since you left Sardinia.' Santino regarded her with cool, questioning expectancy.

'Supporting…*me*?' Frankie repeated in a tone of complete amazement. *'You?'*

'I was expecting Diamond Lil to show up at the La Rocca hotel. The little Fiat was a surprise. A chauffeur-driven limo would have been more appropriate,' Santino mused silkily.

Frankie released a shaken laugh. 'I don't know what you're talking about. I've been working for the past three years. I support myself. I have never received any money from you.'

Santino spread fluently expressive lean brown hands. 'If that is true, it would appear that *someone* has committed fraud on an extensive scale since we last met.'

Her lashes fluttering in bemusement, Frankie studied him closely. He didn't look as angry as he should have done, she thought dazedly. 'Fraud?' she repeated jerkily, the very seriousness of such a crime striking her. 'But who…? I mean, how was the money paid?'

'Through your solicitor.'

'Gosh, he must be a real crook,' Frankie mumbled, feeling suddenly weaker than ever, her limbs almost literally weighted to the bed. Santino had been paying money towards her support all these years? Even though she hadn't received a penny of it, she was shattered by the news. Feeling as she did about him, she would never have accepted his money. He owed her nothing. In fact she felt really humiliated by the idea that he had thought he did have some sort of obligation towards her.

'Forse…perhaps, but let us not leap to conclusions,' Santino murmured, strangely detached from the news that someone had been ripping him off for years.

Frankie was thinking back to that one meeting she had had with ancient old Mr Sweetberry in his cluttered, dingy office. He had looked like a character out of a Charles Dickens novel, only lacking a pair of fingerless gloves. When he had realised that her marriage had taken place in a foreign country, he had looked very confused, as if it hadn't previously occurred to him that people *could* get married outside the UK. In fact he had reacted with a blankness which hadn't impressed Frankie at all. Her mother had then pointed out that Mr Sweetberry didn't charge much for his services and that they could not afford to be too choosy.

'Possibly,' Santino remarked, 'the guilty party might have been someone rather closer than your solicitor...'

Someone in Sardinia, someone on *his* side of the fence, she gathered he meant. Enormous relief swept over her, her own sense of responsibility eased by the idea. She felt incredibly tired but she still felt that she had to say it again. 'I really wouldn't have taken your money, Santino.'

Santino sent her a winging smile, alive with so much natural charisma that her heartbeat skidded into acceleration. 'I believe you,' he said quietly. 'But the culprit must be apprehended, do you not think?'

'Of course,' Frankie eagerly agreed, grateful that he had accepted that she was telling the truth but still highly embarrassed by the situation he had outlined.

Without warning a sinking sensation then afflicted her stomach. All of a sudden she understood why Santino had been so determined to see her. He had obviously needed to talk about this money thing! She was mortified. She might pretty much loathe her ex-husband, but the knowledge that he had been shelling out for years in the belief that he was maintaining her could only make her feel guilty as hell. Had he found it difficult to keep up the payments? The quip about Diamond Lil suggested Santino *had* found it a burden. Frankie wanted to cringe.

'And this greedy, dishonest individual—you...er... think this person should be pursued by the full weight of the law?'

Frankie groaned. 'What's the matter with you? I never thought you'd be such a wimp! Whoever's responsible should be charged, prosecuted and imprisoned. In fact I won't be at peace until I know he's been punished, because this fraud has been committed in *my* name…and I feel awful about it!'

'Not like hitting me any more?'

'Well, not right now,' Frankie muttered grudgingly.

Santino straightened the lace-edged sheet and smoothed her pillows. She didn't notice.

'If only you had explained right at the beginning,' she sighed, feeling suddenly very low in spirits. 'I suppose this is why you invited me to stay. You needed to talk about the money—'

'I am ashamed to admit that I believed that you might have been party to the fraud.'

'I understand,' she allowed, scrupulously fair on the issue, and then, just as she was on the very edge of sleep, another more immediate anxiety occurred to her. 'You'd better have me moved to another room, Santino…'

'Why?'

'My insurance won't pay out for this kind of luxury—'

'Don't worry about it. You will not have to make a claim.'

Santino had such a wonderfully soothing voice, she reflected, smothering a rueful yawn. 'I don't want you paying the bill either.'

'There won't be one…at least…not in terms of cash,' Santino mused softly.

'Sorry?'

'Go to sleep, *cara*.'

Abstractedly, just before she passed over the brink into sleep, she wondered how on earth Santino had produced that wedding photograph in a convent infirmary wing, but it didn't seem terribly important, and doubtless there was a perfectly reasonable explanation. After all, she now knew exactly *why* Santino believed that they were still married. The perpetrator of the financial fraud had naturally decided to keep him in the dark about the annulment so that he would continue to pay.

The sun was high in the sky when Frankie woke up again. She slid out of bed. Apart from a dull ache still lingering at the base of her skull, she now felt fine. She explored the adjoining bathroom with admiring eyes. The fitments were quite sinfully luxurious. This was definitely not a convent infirmary wing. She was amused by her own foolish misapprehension of before. She was so obviously staying in a top-flight hotel! She reached for the wrapped toothbrush awaiting her and then stilled again.

Had this been Santino's room? Had he given it up for her benefit? Was that why the photo had been sitting out? Why would Santino be carrying a framed photograph of their wedding around with him this long after the event? She frowned, her mouth tightening. She could think of only one good reason. And her mouth compressed so hard and flat, it went numb. Masquerading as a safely married man might well prevent his lovers from getting the wrong idea about the level of his commitment, she conceded in disgust. But then if Santino had genuinely believed that he *was* still a married man…?

That odd sense of depression still seemed to be hanging over her. She couldn't understand it. Naturally she was upset that Santino should've assumed that she was happily living high off the fat of the land on his money, but she knew that she was not *personally* responsible for the fraud he had suffered. And he had believed her, hadn't he? He also had to be greatly relieved to know that he wouldn't have to pay another penny.

Diamond Lil… Just how much cash had he consigned into the black hole of someone else's clever little fraud? Weren't people despicable? All of a sudden she felt very sorry for Santino but ever so slightly superior. Evidently

he wasn't half as sharp as he looked or he would have
put some check on his method of payment.

Her suitcase was sitting in the corner of the bedroom.
As she dressed, she sighed. Santino must have been desperate to sort out this money business to go to the
lengths of pretending that he wanted her to come and
stay with him. Why would he have been staying in a
hotel, though, if his home was nearby? And this was
some hotel. How could he possibly afford a room like
this? Unless this wasn't a hotel but was, in fact,
Santino's *home*...

Frankie laughed out loud at that ridiculous idea even
though her grandfather, Gino, had told her smugly that
Santino was rich and a very good catch. In her eyes too,
then, Santino had seemed rich. He had bought the largest
house in Sienta for their occupation—an old farmhouse
on the outskirts of the village. He had even carted a
fancy washing machine home to her one weekend. Not
that she had done much with it. She hadn't understood
the instructions and, after flooding the kitchen several
times, she had merely pretended that she was using it.
Of course, Santino had not seemed rich simply because
he could afford a house and a car! He had just been
considerably better off than anyone else in Sienta.

So therefore this *had* to be a hotel. Without further
waste of time, Frankie pulled on loden-green cotton trousers and a toning waistcoat-style top with half-sleeves
before she plaited her fiery hair. She discovered two new
freckles on the bridge of her classic nose and scowled
as she closed her case again, ready for her departure. A
knock sounded on the door. A uniformed chambermaid
entered with a breakfast tray and then shyly removed
herself again. There was no hovering for a tip either.

While she ate with appetite, Frankie found her eyes
returning again and again to that silver-framed photo sitting on the dressing table. Finally she leapt up and
placed it face-down. Why had Santino kissed her yes-

terday? she suddenly asked herself. Curiosity now that
she had grown up? Or had he actually started fancying
her five years too late? Had her cold and businesslike
attitude to him stung that all-male ego of his? Had he
expected her still to blush and simper and gush over him
the way she had as a teenager?

Frankie shuddered with retrospective chagrin, only
wishing she had found some of that defensive distance
in Santino's arms. But, as for what she had *imagined*
she felt, hadn't she once been hopelessly infatuated with
Santino? Doubtless that adolescent memory had heavily
influenced her response. For a few dangerous seconds,
the years had slipped back and she had felt like that love-
lorn teenager again, a helpless victim of emotions and
longings too powerful for her to control.

And if Frankie went back in time she could easily
remember a much younger Santino, a tall, graceful,
golden-skinned youth, who had looked startlingly akin
to some pagan god of myth and legend. He had only
been twenty then, still a student. While he was visiting
his great-uncle, Father Vassari, the elderly priest had
brought him to her grandfather's house purely because
Santino spoke English and nobody else in the village
did.

In those early days Frankie had picked up little of the
ancient Latin-based dialect her grandfather and his sisters, Maddalena and Teresa, had spoken within their tiny
home. After months of isolation, the sound of her own
language had released a flood of tears and frantic,
over-emotional speech from her. She had begged
Santino to find out where her father was and when he
was returning to take her back to England.

He had suggested that they go for a walk. 'I am not
going to talk to you as if you are a little girl,' Santino
had told her wryly. 'I will be frank. Father Vassari be-
lieves that you will be happier if you learn to accept that

this village is now your home, for the foreseeable future at least.'

Scanning her shocked face, he had emitted a rueful sigh. 'He understands that this life is not what you have been accustomed to and that you find your lack of freedom stifling, but you too must understand that your grandfather is unlikely to change his attitudes—'

'I hate him!' Frankie had gasped helplessly. 'I hate everyone here!'

'But you have your father's blood in your veins, and therefore your grandfather's too,' Santino had reminded her, endeavouring to reason her out of her passionate bitterness and homesickness. 'Gino acknowledges that bond. If he did not, he would not have accepted you into his home. You are part of his family—'

'They're *not* my family!' she had sobbed wretchedly.

'Maddalena would be very hurt to hear you say that. She seems to be very fond of you.'

Her shy great-aunt, who was wholly dominated by her sharp-tongued elder sister and her quick-tempered brother, had been the only member of the household to make any effort to ease Frankie's misery. She had never shouted at Frankie when she heard her crying in the night. She had quietly attempted to offer what comfort she could.

'I promise that I will try to locate your father, but in return you must make a promise to me,' Santino had informed her gravely. 'A promise you must study to keep for your own sake.'

'What kind of promise?'

'Stop running away. It only makes your grandfather angrier, only convinces him that you have been very badly brought up and cannot be trusted out of the house. He is a strict man, and your continued defiance makes him much nastier than he would normally be—'

'Did Father Vassari say Grandfather was nasty?' Frankie had prompted, wide-eyed.

'Of course not.' Santino had flushed slightly. 'But Gino Caparelli has the reputation of being a stubborn, unyielding man. What you must do is bite your tongue in his presence and appear willing to do as you're told, even if you don't feel willing—'

'I bet the priest never told you to tell me to act like a hypocrite!'

'You're smart for a twelve-year-old!' Santino had burst out laughing when she'd caught him out. 'My great-uncle is very devout, but he *is* sincerely concerned by your unhappiness. He wanted me to tell you to respect and obey your grandfather in all things—'

'But you didn't say that—'

'Where there is as yet no affection, I think it would be too much to ask of you.'

'I just want to go back to London,' she had mumbled, the tears threatening again. 'To my mum...my friends, my school—'

'But for now you must learn to live with the Sardinian half of your family, *piccola mia*,' Santino had told her ruefully.

He had been so straight with her and, after long, frightening months of being treated like an impertinent child whose needs and wishes were of no account, she had been heartened by Santino's level approach. But then he had been clever. He had known how to win a respectful hearing, and the bait he had dangled in reward for improved behaviour had convinced her that he was on her side. She had trusted him to find out where her father was.

When he had brought instead the news of her father's death in a car crash, she had been devastated. But, in the years which had followed, Santino had become Frankie's lifeline. He had visited his great-uncle every couple of months, more often as the old man's health had begun to fail, and Frankie had learnt to live for Santino's visits for he always made time for her as well.

She had had nothing in common with her father's family. It had been an unimaginable joy and relief to talk without fear of censure to Santino and just be herself. He had sent her English books and newspapers to read and she had started writing to him. His brief letters had kept her going between visits. Learning to love and rely on Santino had come so naturally to her.

As she dredged herself out of the past, Frankie found poignant memories of Gino, Maddalena and Teresa threatening to creep up out of her subconscious. Stiffening, she closed her Sard relatives out of her mind again. Her grandfather had ignored her letters in the last five years and that hadn't been a surprise. He could neither have understood nor condoned the actions of a granddaughter who had deserted her husband. Her father's family had thought the sun rose and set on Santino. In their ignorance of the true state of his marriage, they would have been angry and bitterly ashamed of her behaviour.

Frankie left her room. She emerged into a panelled corridor, lined with dark medieval paintings and beautiful rugs that glowed with the dull richness of age. When she saw a stone spiral staircase twisting up out of sight at the foot of the passageway, she was tempted to explore. Well, why not? If the villas on the Costa Smeralda were not to be made available to the agency, she was now technically on holiday. She really ought to give Matt a call, she conceded absently. He might be wondering why he hadn't heard from her in three days.

Through the studded oak door at the top of the spiral flight of steps, Frankie stepped out onto the roof...or was it the ramparts? With astonished eyes, she scanned the big square towers rising at either end and then, walking over to the parapet, she gazed down in dizzy horror at the sheerness of the drop, where ancient stone met cliff-face far below her, and then she looked up and around, drinking in the magnificent views of the snow-capped mountains that surrounded the fertile wooded valley.

'You seem to have made a good recovery.'

Frankie very nearly jumped out of her skin. Breathlessly she spun round. Santino was strolling towards her and this time he looked disturbingly familiar. Faded blue jeans sheathed his lean hips and long, powerful thighs, a short-sleeved white cotton shirt was open at his strong brown throat. He walked like the king of the jungle on the prowl, slow, sure-footed and very much a predator.

Sexy, she thought dizzily, struggling weakly to drag her disobedient gaze from his magnificent physique. Incredibly sexy. He was so flagrantly at home with his very male body, relaxed, indolent, staggeringly self-assured. She reddened furiously as he paused several feet away. He sank down with careless grace on the edge of the parapet, displaying the kind of complete indifference to the empty air and the terrifying drop behind him that brought Frankie out in a cold sweat.

'I saw you from the tower. I thought you'd still be in bed,' he admitted.

'I'm pretty resilient,' Frankie returned stiffly, thinking that it would mean little to her if he went over the edge but, all the same, she wished he would move.

'One committed career woman, no less,' Santino drawled, running diamond-bright dark eyes consideringly over the plain businesslike appearance she had contrived to present in spite of the heat. 'To think you used to wash my shirts and shrink them.'

Frankie was maddened by the further flush of embarrassment that crept up her throat. It reminded her horribly of the frightful adolescent awkwardness she had once exhibited around Santino. Not that that surprised her. Santino was drop-dead gorgeous. Santino would make a Greek god look plain and homely because he had a quality of blazing vibrance and energy that no statue could ever match. If she hadn't fancied him like mad all those years ago, there would have been something lacking in her teenage hormones, she told herself.

'Did I really?' she said in a flat, bored tone.

'I always wondered if you boiled them,' Santino mused, perversely refusing to take the hint that the subject was a conversation-killer.

'Well, you should have complained if it bothered you.'

'You were a marvellous cook.'

'I enjoyed cooking for you about as much as I enjoyed scrubbing your kitchen floor!' And she was lying; she hated the fact that she was lying and that, worst of all, he had to know that she was lying.

But what else had she known? The formal education she had received from the age of eleven had been minimal, but her domestic training as a future wife and mother had been far more thorough. Between them, her father's family had seen to that. No matter how hard she had fought to preserve her own identity, she had in the end been indoctrinated with prehistoric ideas of a woman's subservient place in the home. Endless backbreaking work and catering to some man's every wish as though he were an angry god to be appeased rather than an equal... That was what she had been taught and that was what she had absorbed as her former life in London had begun to take on the shadowy and meaningless unreality of another world.

Her spine notched up another inch, bitter resentment at what she had been reduced to steeling her afresh. She had *sung* as she scrubbed his kitchen floor! She had thought she knew it all by then. She had thought that by marrying Santino, who said 'please' and 'thank you' and even, amazingly, 'That's too heavy for you to carry,' she had beaten the system, but in truth she had joined it. She had been prepared to settle for whatever she could get if she could have Santino. For the entire six months of their marriage, she would not have accepted a plane ticket out of Sardinia had it been forced on her...

'I did try to persuade you to resume your education,' he reminded her drily.

'Oh, keep quiet...stop dragging it all back up. It makes me feel ill!' Frankie snapped, spinning away with smarting eyes.

He had wanted her to attend a further education college in Florence. *Florence!* The Caparellis had been aghast when she'd mentioned it. What kind of a husband sent his wife back to school? She could read, she could write, she could count—what more did he want? And Frankie had been genuinely terrified of being sent away to a strange city where her ignorance would be exposed, where the other students might laugh at her poor Italian and where, worst of all, she would not have Santino.

In her innocence, she had actually asked Santino if he would go to Florence with her, and he had said that he would only be able to visit because the demands of his job would not allow him to live there. Of course, in the kindest possible way, she conceded grudgingly, Santino had been trying to make the first step towards loosening the ties of their ridiculous marriage by persuading her into a separation and a measure of independence. He had known very well that she was so infatuated with him that she was unlikely to make a recovery as long as he was still around.

He hadn't wanted to hurt her. He had even said that, yes, he would miss her very much but that he felt that she would greatly gain in self-confidence if she completed her education. And she had accused him then of being ashamed of her and had raced upstairs in floods of inconsolable tears. She had refused to eat for the rest of that weekend, had alternately sulked and sobbed every time he'd tried to reason with her. No, she reflected painfully, nobody could ever say that Santino had found marriage to his child-bride a bed of roses…or, indeed, any kind of a bed at all, she conceded with burning cheeks.

'We have a lot to talk about,' Santino commented flatly.

Tension hummed in the air. For the first time, Frankie became aware of that thick tension and frowned at the surprising coldness she was only now registering in Santino's voice. Before, Santino had been teasing her, yet now he was undeniably distant and cool. She didn't know him in this mood. The awareness disconcerted her and then made her angrily defensive.

'On a personal basis we have nothing to talk about, but good luck with your fraud case!' Frankie told him with a ferociously bright smile. 'However, if you want to discuss the—'

'If you mention those villas one more time, I will lose my temper. What are they to me? Nothing,' Santino derided with a dismissive gesture of one lean hand. 'The bait by which I brought you here, but now no more! Their role is played now.'

'I'm afraid I haven't a clue what more you expect from me, and nor do I intend to hang around to find out,' Frankie asserted, colliding with hard golden eyes that were curiously chilling, and, since that was not a sensation which she had ever associated with Santino before, she paled and tensed up even more.

'You will. Your wings are now clipped. No longer will you fly free,' Santino retorted with the cool, clear diction generally reserved for a child slow of understanding. 'We are still married.'

'Why do you keep on saying that?' Frankie demanded in sudden flaring repudiation. 'It's just not true!'

'Five years ago you made only a brief initial statement to your solicitor, who has since retired. I spoke to his son yesterday. He checked the files for me. His father advised you in a letter to consult another solicitor, one more experienced in the matrimonial field. No further action was taken,' he completed drily.

Frankie trembled. There was something horribly convincing about Santino's growing impatience with her. 'If there's been some stupid oversight, I'm sorry, and I promise that I'll take care of it as soon as I go home again—'

'Not on the grounds of non-consummation!' Santino slotted in grimly.

'Any grounds you like, for goodness' sake...I'm not fussy,' Frankie muttered, badly shaken by the idea that they might still be legally married.

'Five years ago I would have agreed to an annulment.' Santino surveyed her tense face with cool, narrowed eyes. 'Indeed, then I considered it my duty to set you free. But that is not a duty which I recognise now. To be crude, Francesca...I now want the wife that I paid for.'

'That you...what?' Frankie parroted shakily.

'I now intend to take possession of what I paid for. That is my right.'

Frankie uttered a strangled laugh that fell like a brick in the rushing silence. She stared at him incredulously. 'You're either crazy or joking...you've *got* to be joking!'

'Why?' Santino scanned her with fulminating dark golden eyes. 'Let's drop the face-saving euphemisms. For a start, you trapped me into marriage.'

Frankie flinched visibly. 'I didn't—'

Santino dealt her a quelling glance. 'Don't dare to deny it. Well do I recall your silence when you were questioned by your grandfather. I had never in my life laid a finger upon you but not one word did you say to that effect!'

Frankie studied the ground, belated shame rising inexorably to choke her. She had been so furious with Santino that awful night for taking her back to Sienta.

She had been running away and, using him as an un-suspecting means of escape, had hidden herself behind the rear seat of his car. It had been an impulsive act, prompted by pure desperation…

Santino's great-uncle, Father Vassari, had died that week. She had known that Santino would no longer have any reason to come to the village. She had been in disgrace on the home front too. Incapable of hiding her feelings for Santino, she had stirred up the sort of malicious local gossip that enraged her grandfather. Furious with her, he had told her that she could no longer even write to Santino.

Santino hadn't discovered her presence in his car until he'd stopped for petrol on the coast. It had been the one and only time he had ever lost his temper with her. His sheer fury had crushed her. Deaf to her every plea for understanding and assistance, he had stuffed her forcibly back into the car and driven her all the way back home, but it had been dawn by the time they got there. In Gino Caparelli's eyes, her overnight absence in male company had ruined her reputation beyond all possibility of redemption. He had instantly demanded that Santino do the honourable thing and marry her.

'Grandfather *knew* nothing had happened,' Frankie began in a wobbly voice, struggling to find even a weak line of self-defence.

'And I knew that after what you had done your life would be hell in that house if I *didn't* marry you! I let conscience persuade me that you were my responsibility. And what did I receive in return?' Santino prompted witheringly. 'A bride who took her teddy bear to bed…'

Frankie's colour was now so high, she was convinced it would take Arctic snow to cool her down again.

'Hamish the teddy with the tartan scarf.' Santino studied her with grim amusement. 'Believe me, he was a hundred times more effective than any medieval chastity belt.'

Intense chagrin flooded her. Her teeth gritted as she threw her head high. 'You said...you said that you wanted a wife—'

'I already have one. I also have custody of Hamish,' Santino informed her satirically as he rose fluidly upright again. 'I'd say that makes my claim indisputable.'

'You don't have any claim over me!'

'Have you packed?' Meeting her stunned scrutiny, Santino repeated his question.

'Yes, but—'

'*Bene*...then, since you are no longer in need of further rest, we will waste no more time.' Santino opened the oak door and, standing back, regarded her expectantly.

The tip of Frankie's tongue slid out to wet her lower lip. She continued to stare helplessly at him. 'Why are you doing this...? I mean, what's going on?'

'Really, Francesca...are you always this slow on the uptake?' Santino chided, an ebony brow elevating with sardonic cool. 'You really shouldn't have lied to me.'

'L-lied?' Frankie stammered as he pressed her firmly past him and down the spiral stone steps. 'I haven't told you any lies!'

'I would have been far more understanding if you had made a complete confession when I confronted you. But lies make me incredibly angry,' Santino drawled softly. 'When I found out the truth this morning, I was very tempted to come upstairs, tip you out of that bed and shake you until the teeth rattled in your calculating, devious little head!'

'What are you talking about?' Frankie exclaimed.

'Your forty-eight per cent share of Finlay Travel.' Santino shot her a glittering look of condemnation from icy cold dark eyes. 'You shameless little bitch... You actually fished your lover out of a financial hole with *my* money!'

Frankie was so taken aback by that insane accusation, she could only gape at him.

'Now, I didn't expect to receive my bride back in a state of untouched virginal purity. Nor did I expect to be greeted with open arms, gratitude or any lingering delusion on your part that I could walk on water!' Santino spelt out with sizzling derision. 'Indeed, I believed that my expectations were thoroughly realistic. But I was *not* prepared to discover that for the past five years you've been in collusion with that greedy, grasping vixen who brought you into the world!'

CHAPTER THREE

FRANKIE tried to swallow and failed. In shock, she had fallen still. Santino was talking about her mother. He was calling Della a greedy, grasping vixen. Why? For heaven's sake, he didn't even know her mother, had never met her!

Why on earth was he making such wild and offensive accusations? It made no sense. She had bought her share of Finlay Travel with the proceeds of an insurance policy. Bewildered green eyes clung to his hard, sun-bronzed features and the cold, steely anger simmering in the depths of his contemptuous gaze.

'When I think of the lengths I went to in my efforts to protect you from having your illusions about Della shattered, I am even more disgusted by your behaviour!' He flung wide the door of her bedroom and crossed the floor to lift her case. Emerging again, he curved a powerful arm against her tense spine and carried her towards the stone staircase that wound impressively down into a big hall. '*Dio mio*...I had to pay your mother to take you back. I had to bribe her to welcome you into her home after you left me!'

'P-pay her...you had to *pay* her?' Frankie repeated in disbelief.

Santino released his breath in an audible hiss. 'I should have insisted on an immediate annulment. I should not have allowed myself to be swayed by the assurance that it would distress you too much to have that last link severed—'

'Distress me...?' Frankie broke in even more shakily as she came to a halt on the uneven flagstoned floor of the hall. Her legs felt appallingly weak and hollow. *Pay her?* He had had to pay her mother? Perspiration dampened her short upper lip. She couldn't get her thoughts into any kind of order. When she continued to hover, Santino pressed her out through the big oak doors spread wide on the brilliant sunlight. Without that forceful male momentum Frankie would very probably have fallen at his feet.

'I was a complete fool,' Santino grated. 'Without question I paid out a vast amount of money for you to live in comfort and complete your education, and what have I got back? A wife who still speaks Italian like a tourist with a bad phrasebook! But that is the very least of the deception, is it not? You're so appallingly mercenary, you chose to live in sin with your lover sooner than give me *my* freedom back!'

'Santino—' Frankie mumbled dizzily.

'Keep quiet. The less I hear out of that lying little mouth right now the better!' Santino cut in with ruthless bite. 'I let myself be taken in yesterday. "Are you in the tourist trade now?" *Dio mio*...give me strength! But I thought, That is *so* sweet. She still doesn't know who I am... But that charade about there being a bill for your medical care—that was overkill! You know damned well you married a bloody rich man! Only a bloody rich man could have kept you and your mother in the style in which I have kept you both for the past five years!'

With that final ringing and derisive assurance, Santino yanked open the door of the black Toyota Landcruiser parked in the cobbled courtyard, and while she stood there in a speechless daze at all the revelations being hurled at her at once he swore with impatience. Circling her with strong arms, he swept her bodily off her feet and, after settling her into the passenger seat, he slammed the door on her.

Frankie found herself sucking in oxygen as frantically

as someone coming up for air after almost drowning.
She pressed trembling fingers to her throbbing temples.

'So don't look at me with those big green eyes and
tell me I'm joking when I say I intend to have what I
paid for!' Santino continued fiercely as he swung in beside her. 'One more argument out of you and I pull the
rug out from under Finlay Travel and ruin both you and
your lover! And then I take Della to court for all the
fake bills that have been submitted on your behalf while
I was still under the impression that you were a student.
By the time I'm finished with you, the sight of a Vitale
bank draft with my signature on it will make you feel
sick. I'm going to treat you to aversion therapy!'

Frankie was fighting to reason again, but she was in
so much shock it was extraordinarily difficult. Somehow
she couldn't get past that very first devastatingly painful
assurance that he had had to pay her mother to give her
a home. 'You've...you've actually met Della?' she
heard herself question weakly but incredulously as he
fired the engine of the powerful car.

'What sort of stupid question is that?' Santino shot
her a glinting glance of enquiry. A sardonic frown line
divided his ebony brows as he absorbed her stark pallor.
'Of course you know I've met her! Don't tell me that
while the two of you were cheerfully ripping me off all
these years she somehow neglected to mention where all
the money was coming from!'

'Mum received a very generous divorce settlement
from her second husband,' Frankie mumbled tremu-
lously, her throat convulsing as she tried to steady herself. 'That's where the money was coming from, and as
for my share in Finlay—'

'Your mother dumped Giles Jensen when his night-
club went bust. He didn't have the means to make *any*
kind of settlement. When you went back home to Mum,
she was in major debt. I was the sucker who pulled Mum
out of it and put a roof over your heads!'

'I don't—'

A plastic folder landed squarely on her lap. 'I own your mother's home. I had no objection to maintaining my mother-in-law when it meant that you shared her comfortable lifestyle. I'm angry now because it's obvious that you were in on the whole scam from the beginning!'

There was a thick legal deed inside the folder. It bore the address of her mother's smart house in Kensington and Santino's name as the current owner. It was the kind of irrefutable proof that stole the very breath from her lungs. It made argument on that count impossible. Her stomach succumbed to nauseous cramps.

'If there hadn't been a recent query about the lease, I wouldn't even have had that here to show you!' Santino gritted. 'But I have a stack of receipted bills a foot thick in my office in Rome. Fakes! Tell me, did you ever actually go to that fancy boarding school I paid for?'

'I went to the local tech for a while, took a few classes…' Frankie told him numbly as the horror of what he was telling her and the source of his very real anger began slowly and inexorably to sink in.

'*Per meraviglia*…no riding, music and skiing lessons? No language tutoring? No finishing school? No educational trips or vacations abroad? You haven't spent a single term at university, have you?'

Dully, Frankie shook her head. Piece by awful piece, it was falling into place. Della was the fraudster Santino had been talking about. Not someone on his side of the fence, but someone a great deal closer to Frankie than a solicitor she had only once met. Her mother, her *own* mother. She felt sick. Della enjoyed an entirely hedonistic existence of shopping and socialising. She didn't work. She had an exquisitely furnished house, a fabulous designer wardrobe and took frequent long-haul holidays abroad. The realisation that Santino must have been paying for that lifestyle devastated Frankie.

'I didn't know...you've got to believe that!' she burst out.

'Fine. Then you can sit back and relax while I prosecute your mother for misuse of funds intended to be spent solely for your benefit.'

Frankie went white.

'And I eagerly await your explanation for the thousands *you* put into Finlay Travel—'

'That *definitely* wasn't your money!' she protested feverishly. 'That came from an insurance policy that Dad took out for Mum and I when I was still a baby—'

'Marco, the compulsive gambler, took out insurance?' Santino murmured very drily. 'Money burned a hole in his pocket. If your father had taken out a policy like that, he would have been trying to cash it in again within months. He certainly wouldn't have kept up the payments.'

Frankie was concentrating hard now. She had never seen any proof that that money had come from an insurance pay-out. She had been only eighteen, had had no reason to question her mother's story or the welcome feeling of security created by that most unexpected windfall. Della had simply paid the money into her account. And by the passing on of that one very substantial payment, Frankie registered painfully, Della had ensured that her daughter was bound up in her dishonesty. Had that been her mother's intention all along? A safeguard so that if Santino ever found out what was really happening to his money he would believe that Frankie had been involved in the deception? Her stomach gave another horrible twist.

'You see, at first I *did* believe that you were telling me the truth. I believed that you had been blissfully unaware of my financial backing until I found out about your stake in Finlay Travel. I was annoyed that you didn't appear to have enjoyed the material and educational benefits that I had believed I was paying for, but

I could have lived with that. What I will not accept with
good grace is that you are as big a cheat and a thief as
your mother!'

'Stop the car…I feel sick!' Frankie suddenly gasped
in desperation.

She almost fell out of the four-wheel drive in her haste
to vacate it. As she gulped in fresh air and swayed, she
hung onto the car door.

'You do look rough,' Santino acknowledged grudgingly as he strode round the bonnet. 'I thought it was a
ruse.'

Frankie couldn't even bring herself to look at him. As
the nervous cramps began to settle in her stomach, she
was wondering sickly just how much cash Della had
contrived to run through in five long years. Given an
inch, Della would have taken a mile. Indeed, she wondered if her mother's demands had grown so excessive
that Santino had finally become suspicious.

'Sit down…' Lean, surprisingly gentle hands detached
her from the death-grip she had on the door and settled
her very carefully back into the passenger seat. 'Put your
head down if you still feel dizzy,' he urged, retaining a
firm grip on her trembling hands when she tried to pull
away.

She focused on his hand-stitched Italian loafers and
slowly breathed in again.

'Better?' Santino prompted flatly, releasing her from
his hold.

Dully, she nodded, glancing up unwarily to collide
with brilliant dark eyes fringed by luxuriant spiky black
lashes. Close up, those eyes had the most extraordinary
effect on her. They made her feel all weak…and sort of
quivery deep down inside. Without even realising it, she
was staring like a mesmerised rabbit, and then Santino
vaulted lithely upright again, leaving her looking
dazedly into space.

Had the shock of her mother's deceit deranged her

wits? she asked herself angrily. What was the matter with her? If there had ever been a time she needed to concentrate, this was it. So Santino was still possessed of spectacular good looks; surely she was mature enough to handle that without behaving in the midst of a crisis like an adolescent with an embarrassing crush?

He owned Della's house, she reminded herself in desperation, so most probably all the rest of it was true as well. Then by rights her share in Finlay Travel belonged to Santino. She could sign it over to him, but it would still only be a tenth of what was owed. And wasn't she in many ways responsible for what her mother had done?

If she hadn't been so willing to believe her mother's assurance that the annulment had been a mere technicality, if she hadn't been too ridiculously sensitive to even want to discuss or be forced to think about her marriage, Della wouldn't have found it so easy to fool her. They would have got that annulment years ago, Santino would have had his freedom back and he would have stopped supporting her mother and herself. But had Frankie asked him to support them? Resentment stirred in her. She had wanted *nothing* from Santino!

'You seem to think you own me, and now I know why.' A jagged little laugh fell from her lips as Santino drove on. 'Well, I'm sorry, but you can't buy people—'

'No, it's love you can't buy. Buying people is surprisingly easy,' Santino drawled. 'You only need to know what they want to hook them.'

Frankie shivered and shot a helpless glance at his lean, dark profile, the hardness of his jawline. 'And what do I want?'

'Most?' Santino queried softly, reflectively. 'To be loved. I saw that in you when you were no age at all. You had a desperate need to be loved. But you were so stubborn you looked for it in the wrong places and couldn't recognise it when you did find it.'

Frankie lost colour. He had answered her ironic question seriously, cutting her to the heart by reminding her of the all too many disappointments and rejections of her growing-up years.

'That's one reason why I certainly wasn't expecting to meet an angel yesterday. A lot of people in your life have let you down. I knew that I, too, had lost your trust, but somehow I still expected you to be the extremely honest girl you used to be. I should have known that Della would mess you up—'

'Don't talk about my mother like that!' Frankie bit out defensively.

'I think it's time someone did. You moved in with Finlay when you were…what…only eighteen years old?'

'Where did you get that information from?' Her voice shook.

'It wasn't difficult. Finlay…' he murmured again. 'Tell me, when you sank that money into his business, were you trying to buy his affection?'

Frankie went rigid. 'How dare—?'

'I've never believed in avoiding the issue. It's a reasonable question. Most teenagers with a large sum of money in their possession could think of a hundred things to do with it, but not one of those hundred exciting possibilities would entail investment.'

Frankie pinned her lips together tightly, reluctant to reply. She had wanted to do something secure with that windfall. Until she had married Santino, every person she had ever depended on had lived on a frightening financial seesaw. Her parents had had violent arguments about money. One day it had been treats all round, the next bitter dispute over an unpaid bill. She had gone from that to the very real poverty of her grandfather's home, where there had been absolutely nothing to spare for extras. And those 'extras' had been everyday necessities which she had taken for granted in London.

'So you *were* buying him—'

'No, I blasted well wasn't!' Frankie flared. 'I even took some advice before I did it.'

'Finlay's advice? I ask because that investment is anything but safe right now. You're in a crowded market and the travel agency is financially over-extended.'

'I'm quite content with the returns I've received—'

'A place in his bed that isn't exclusively yours? I know you're not the only woman in his life...'

Frankie was becoming angrier and angrier with every second that passed. 'Well, maybe he's not the only man in mine.'

'Few women settle for an open relationship at your age. Are you that much in love with him?'

Frankie abruptly spread both hands in a gesture of furious frustration. 'I am not in love with Matt. We're friends and I'm the junior partner—'

'Why live together, then?'

'I have as much right to live in that apartment as he has, or didn't your snoop tell you that? Finlay Travel owns the building!'

'Correction...the bank owns it.'

'So now *you* have a share of what the bank owns!'

'Smart move, Francesca. I quite understand why your lover has suddenly become your platonic friend. But if you think I intend to move in and refinance your boyfriend you're insane,' Santino asserted very drily. 'That is one ship which will sink without any help from me!'

'Do whatever you like. If it was your money to begin with, it's your investment now! But don't make Matt pay for something that has nothing to do with him,' Frankie argued vehemently. 'The agency needs those villas. He'd have no trouble keeping them fully booked right through the season. We badly need more quality properties.'

Santino vented a distinctly chilling laugh. 'You're unbelievable. You rip me off and then you expect me to come to your assistance?'

'I didn't rip you off…I honestly didn't know about the money… And I don't think it's my fault anyway,' she reasoned with steadily mounting resentment. 'You went behind my back to make some stupid arrangement with Della which *I* didn't know about, so how can you now blame me for it going wrong?'

'*Santo cielo*…the rats are jumping ship fast,' Santino murmured sardonically. 'It would appear that it's every woman for herself now. Don't worry about it. I'm very even-handed when I deal out rough justice. I assure you that Della's getting her share of grief today too.'

Frankie tensed. 'What do you mean?'

'She will be served with an eviction notice by the end of the day.'

Frankie surveyed him in horror. Santino indolently drew the car to a slow halt and climbed out. Frankie leapt out at speed. 'You *can't* do that to her!'

'Give me one good reason why not.'

Frankie hovered on the edge of the dusty road, thinking hard, but her mind was a complete blank. Sheer shock was resounding through her in dizzy waves.

Santino slung her a grimly amused look from veiled golden eyes and calmly removed a basket and a rug from the back of the car. 'It's a challenge, isn't it?' he agreed.

'It's not that… I just can't believe you could be that cruel!' Frankie admitted helplessly.

'But then you've never met with this side of me before. Only with you was I ever a pussycat and, sadly for you, those days are past,' Santino delivered with hard dark eyes that glittered like golden ice in the sunlight. 'I'm lethally unforgiving in business, Francesca…and I'm sorry to say that both you and your unlovely mother fall very much into the category of business now.'

The tip of her tongue snaked out to moisten her dry lower lip in a flicking motion. She just couldn't believe that this was Santino. He was correct about that all right. She didn't recognise the warm, teasing, tolerant male she remembered in this tall dark man with his savagely hard and unfeeling eyes. Her attention fell on the basket he held and total bewilderment seized her. 'What are you doing with that?'

'It's for our picnic,' Santino divulged gently.

Her generous mouth opened and shut. As yet it hadn't even occurred to her to wonder why he had stopped the car and got out.

'Our…picnic?' she questioned unevenly. 'Let me get this straight… Just after you announce that you're having my mother served with an eviction notice, you expect me to join you for a picnic?'

'And the thought of that eviction notice has whetted my appetite,' Santino confided without remorse as he swung fluidly on his heel.

In stunned disbelief Frankie watched him stride down the grassy, rutted track on the far side of the car. It led down the sloping ground into the thick cover of trees. Within a minute, that dark, imperious head was out of sight. Gritting her teeth, Frankie abandoned her pride and chased after him. She passed by the tumbledown shell of a little stone house, long since given over to the weeds and the undergrowth, and just beyond it, beneath the dappled shade of an ancient gnarled tree, she saw that the rug and the basket had been abandoned.

Santino was poised on the brow of the sun-drenched hillside, looking down at the village which straggled untidily over the slopes below them. As she drew level with him, he turned his head.

'Santino,' she began tautly, 'my—'

'That's La Rocca down there,' he cut in informatively. 'My grandmother was born in the bar where we met yesterday. It was called a hotel in those days too. Her father had aspirations which were never fulfilled.'

Frankie frowned uncertainly. 'I—'

'Keep quiet and listen.' Brilliant dark eyes lanced into

hers, his sensual mouth hardening. 'What else can you see from here?'

She swallowed hard and looked around herself with blank, uncomprehending eyes, wondering what on earth he was driving at.

'My grandfather was born in that ruin,' he supplied with studied patience. 'One of eleven children, only six of whom survived to adulthood. He brought me here when I was eight years old and he told me that this is where the Vitale family has its roots. Humble beginnings but, believe it or not, I'm very proud of them.'

'Yes, I can see that,' Frankie muttered abstractedly. 'But—'

'No, you do not *see* at all!' Santino grated with driving derision, and strode away from her.

Frankie just couldn't concentrate; she was too shaken up by all that had burst upon her. Her temples were pounding with tension. But she seemed to be suffering alone, for Santino was uncorking a bottle of wine, his hands deft and sure, stray arrows of light skimming over his chiselled golden profile and the lean, fluid sweep of his lithe masculine body as he knelt on the rug.

'She's got visitors staying right now…Mum, I mean,' she began helplessly, unable even to organise her thoughts, never mind her speech. 'And I'm not trying to excuse what's been done, but she hasn't had it easy—'

'Until *I* came along—'

Frankie flushed and stepped off one foot onto the other. 'She could have been a top model if she hadn't been saddled with me. And then Dad took me and she couldn't find me, and she ended up marrying Giles and he—'

'Was bankrupted by her extravagance.'

Frankie stiffened. 'That's not the way I heard it.'

'I don't suppose she would have told it that way. You're wasting your breath,' Santino informed her drily as he slid upright. 'Della's the very soul of avarice. I

tied her into a strict legal agreement—even then I had
few illusions about her character—and, believe me, she
exercised considerable criminal talent in all the fraudu-
lent claims for cash that were made… You can't expect
me to listen to sob-stories on her behalf when you took
your cut too.'

'Are you planning to prosecute us both?'

'Can you really see me dragging my wife into court?
But your mother…' Santino met her wide, fearful eyes
in a head-on collision that slithered through her like a
hard physical blow. 'I have no inhibitions about punishing her.'

'But if you consider me equally at fault that wouldn't
be fair!' Frankie protested, utterly appalled by the idea
of her mother being taken to court and prosecuted like
a criminal.

'Are you telling me that you were in on it too, from
the start?' Santino demanded very quietly. 'I had received the impression that Della ensured that you
received only a small percentage of the money.'

Frankie's heart was pumping at feverish speed behind
her breastbone. She could hardly breathe. 'I knew exactly what Della was doing *right* from the beginning,'
she lied with fierce emphasis, reasoning that if she forced
him to share out the blame it might somehow lessen his
fury with her mother and persuade him to direct it at her
instead.

Santino was very still, his spectacular bone structure
rigid below his golden skin, his eyes hooded. 'You're
changing your story now?'

'I knew that taking your money was wrong but I…I
hated you after I saw you with that woman in Cagliari!'
Frankie shot her last bolt in her determination to give
her mother what protection she could.

'That I can believe…but I also once believed that you
would sooner starve than knowingly accept my support.
Hence the original secrecy. Was I really that naive?'

Santino surveyed her with narrowed dark eyes of grim
enquiry, his beautiful mouth taking on a uniquely cynical
twist. 'That protective, that romantic? It seems you're
not the only one who needed to grow up five years ago.
I set out to be a hero and fell at the first fence!'

Frankie wasn't listening to him. 'Please don't do this
to Mum,' she whispered pleadingly. 'Give her the time
to move out of the house with dignity—'

'And what would I get in return for such undeserved
restraint?'

The silence lay thick and oppressive in the stillness.
There wasn't the slightest breeze. The heat of midday
was like a cocoon. It dampened her skin beneath her
clothing. As she breathed in deeply, her distraught green
eyes locked into that lancing look of ruthless challenge.

'I don't know what you want...'

'Don't you?' A derisive smile of disagreement twisted
Santino's sensual mouth. 'I want you in my bed.'

'I can't believe that...' Frankie muttered unsteadily,
unable to accept that he could be serious. 'I can't believe
that that's what you want.'

'Isn't that what every man wants from a beautiful
woman?'

'I'm not beautiful—'

Santino advanced in one long, graceful stride. He
stared down at her with brooding dark golden eyes that
burned hotly beneath her skin. And then he lifted his
hands and with cool, deft fingers detached the clip from
her plait. 'I like your hair loose.'

With disturbing patience he threaded out the multiple
strands one by one, and the whole time Frankie stood
there trembling, barely breathing, but with every brush
of those brown fingers against her cheekbone, or her
scalp, or even the nape of her neck, her heart raced faster
and her pulses pounded even harder, leaving her dizzy.

'Very beautiful, very sexy,' Santino stressed huskily
as he drew her closer.

Instantly she tensed, the sun-warmed, eerily familiar male scent of him flaring her nostrils. Her breasts felt languorously full and heavy, the nipples taut buds of swollen sensitivity pushing against the rough cotton that bound them. There was no thought in her dazed mind as she connected with shimmering golden eyes, only a powerful, drugging awareness of every throbbing skin-cell she possessed.

'And so incredibly submissive all of a sudden too. And you might tell yourself it's to save Della from her just deserts, but really that wouldn't be honest, *piccola mia*. There's a streak of wildness in you. There always was,' Santino breathed in a harshly amused undertone as he released her again. 'And right now you're more likely to expire from excitement than petrified reluctance!'

In shock, Frankie fell back from him, outraged by that assurance but silenced by a sudden sense of intense shame as she acknowledged the truth of it. Her own weak body betrayed her with wanton efficiency. For an instant she had wanted him with a desperate physical yearning over which she had absolutely no control. And it had nothing to do with any echo from the past, nothing to do with what she had once felt...it had been an instinctive craving born very much of the present.

Santino bent down and, drawing two glasses from the basket, he passed her one. 'I'm not complaining, you understand,' he murmured smoothly. 'A sacrificial lamb wouldn't appeal to me. But then what you've become doesn't have any *lasting* appeal either...'

Her skin as hot as hellfire, angry pain sparking in a raw surge through her taut length, Frankie stood her ground. 'What are you trying to say?'

'That at this moment I believe three weeks will suit me fine.' Dense black lashes screening his gaze, Santino treated her to a gleaming scrutiny that was coolly derisive. 'Three weeks will be quite long enough.'

Three weeks was the span of the vacation she had planned to spend touring Italy. Her hand shook slightly as he let clear sparkling wine splash down into her glass. 'You're asking me to spend that time with you?'

'Only this time around Hamish gets to sleep alone,' Santino spelt out lazily.

'I had gathered that,' Frankie gritted, but she couldn't meet his eyes.

'At the end of it, we go our separate ways and get a divorce. Della moves out of the house and I wipe the slate clean. It's a very generous offer,' he asserted softly.

It didn't feel generous to Frankie; it felt horribly humiliating and degrading. She recalled the derision in his gaze and shrank inside herself. Santino had seemed almost like a stranger in the café, but that impression had melted away when she'd seen flashes of the Santino she remembered. Only now he was a stranger again.

'The choice is yours.'

'I don't see a choice.' If she didn't stay, he would prosecute Della. She could not bear to think of her mother being dragged through court on a charge of serious fraud, even if that was very probably what she deserved, she allowed painfully. 'I have no option but to agree,' she breathed tightly.

'Don't pluck violin strings,' Santino advised very drily as he dug a mobile phone out of his pocket, punched out a number and proceeded to speak to someone in Italian too fast for her to follow. Retracting the aerial, he slung the phone aside. 'The eviction order will not be served.'

In a silent daze of disbelief at the agreement he had forced on her, Frankie sank clumsily down on the rug and tipped the wine to her parched lips with a trembling hand.

CHAPTER FOUR

A FIRM hand shook Frankie's shoulder and she opened her eyes. The sun had changed position in the sky.

'It's time to leave.' Reaching down to close his hands over hers, Santino pulled her upright with easy strength.

It was afternoon. Her last recollection was of setting down that empty wine glass. She had slept for a couple of hours. Awkwardly smoothing down her creased trousers, Frankie straightened and finger-combed her wildly tumbled hair out of her drowsily bemused eyes. 'Why didn't you wake me up?'

'I assumed that you still needed some extra rest.' Santino swept up the rug and folded it. The picnic basket had already gone.

'Why did you bring me to this place anyway?' Frankie demanded with helpless curiosity.

'Perhaps I was foolishly attempting to resurrect fond memories of the family you abandoned on this island.'

At that charge, Frankie froze in shock. 'I beg y-your pardon?'

'Gino, Maddalena and Teresa,' Santino enumerated with cutting precision. 'Although you have yet to ask, your grandfather and your great-aunts are all alive and well.'

Santino swung fluidly on his heel and strode back up the grassy track towards the road. Turning a furious pink at that censorious assurance, Frankie raced after him. 'I wrote several times and my grandfather never replied once!'

'Don't tell me any more lies,' Santino advised with an icy bite in his tone as she drew level with him. 'You didn't write. I would've been the first to hear of it if you had.'

'I did write...I *did*!' Frankie protested defensively, but then in her mind's eye loomed the memory of Della taking the letters from her and assuring her that *she* would post them. Her heart sank like a stone. Had those stilted communications she had sweated blood and tears over ever been posted? After all, any exchange of news between Frankie and Gino Caparelli might have endangered Della's plans to enrich herself at Santino's expense.

'I bet Mum didn't post my letters!' she exclaimed.

Santino skimmed her a look of silent and crushing contempt.

Frankie turned her head away, conscious that he didn't believe her and that her excuse sounded pitifully weak. Yet she *had* written several times to her Sard relatives. But those first months back in London had also been a period of frightening disorientation and readjustment for Frankie...

Suddenly plunged back into the world her father had taken her from, she had felt utterly lost and had holed herself up in her mother's flat like a wounded animal, surrendering to both depression and self-pity. Finding Santino with that other woman in Cagliari had devastated her. Santino had been her whole world then—the focus of her love and trust, the support she leant on in times of crisis and the source of all her self-confidence.

And then, in one appalling moment of revelation, she had finally been forced to face the demeaning reality that their marriage had never been anything other than a cruelly empty charade and a burden on his side of the fence. Well, no matter how badly Santino thought of her now, she certainly wasn't about to tell him how she had fallen apart after leaving him or how long it had taken her to pull herself back together again!

She climbed into the four-wheel drive. 'A bloody rich

man', he had called himself. Vitale…the bank in
Cagliari… *Vitale*. She could even recall seeing that
name a couple of years ago in a glossy magazine, rec-
ognising it because it had once so briefly been her name
as well. The story had been about a banking family, a
great and legendary Italian banking family, who shielded
their privacy to such an extent that photographs of any
one of them were rare. And that extreme caution had
stemmed from the kidnapping of a family member thirty
years earlier.

Two months after her very first meeting with Santino,
he had come to tell her grandfather that his son,
Frankie's father, Marco, had been killed in a car crash
in Spain. Frankie had been savaged by the news, not
least because by that stage she had begun thinking re-
sentfully of the father who had deserted her as being no
better than a kidnapper. In her guilt-stricken distress, she
had admitted as much to Santino.

'When your father lied to you and told you that he
and your mother were reconciling, when he brought you
here and chose to leave you with a family who were
strangers…*yes*, that was irresponsible, selfish and
wrong,' Santino had responded fiercely. 'But don't you
ever say that you were kidnapped, *piccola mia*. I have
an uncle who many years on still bears the scars of that
crime. Kidnappers are cruel and violent criminals who
deprive innocent people of their freedom for profit!'

Sinking back to the present, Frankie stole a shattered
glance at Santino's hard classic profile as he ignited the
engine of the powerful car and drove off. What was it
he had said earlier? That the sight of a Vitale bank draft
with his signature on it would make her feel sick? He
had also mentioned having an office in Rome.

'Why were you working in that bank in Cagliari?' she
asked in a wobbly voice, because even though she had
had it hurled in her teeth by him already she just found
it so incredibly hard to believe that the man she had

married at sixteen might always have had a life far removed from hers which he'd chosen to keep secret.

'I was the manager there. My father believed that it would be useful practical experience for me before I took my seat on the board. However, he did think that choosing to bury myself in a small branch of our bank in Sardinia was going to severe extremes. But he was not then aware that I had other reasons for making that curious choice of locality...not least a child-bride stashed away in the mountains!'

Our bank. Frankie gulped, realisation dawning. 'And all the time you owned a blasted castle at the other end of the island!'

'I only took possession of the *castello* last year,' Santino contradicted her. 'Before that it belonged to my father, and he had leased it out as a hotel for over twenty years.'

'It doesn't matter. You told me nothing about yourself—'

'I told no lies and I gave you as much information as you could cope with. You were perfectly content within your own little world just playing house. Measure the level of your maturity then by recalling how much you ever asked me about what I actually *did* for a living,' Santino suggested drily. 'As I remember it, your sole angle of interest then was that working kept me away from you all week!'

Flames of mortified colour burnished Frankie's complexion. 'What was I supposed to ask you? I'd never been in a bank in my life and I just didn't want to expose my ignorance! Look, where are we going?' she demanded abruptly. 'This isn't the way we came—'

'We're heading to Sienta for a long-awaited Caparelli family reunion,' Santino delivered levelly.

At the news that they were heading for her grandfather's village, Frankie's soft mouth dropped open. *'Sienta?'* she gasped strickenly.

'I hope your family never learn that you would've come to Sardinia and left again without even treating them to a brief visit—'

'Damn you...don't you dare turn pious on me!' Frankie flared back at him in furious reproof. 'You know better than anyone how miserable I was in that village! My grandfather could've written to my mother at any time and she would've flown over and taken me home, but she never got the chance because she didn't know where I was...'

Santino drew the car to a halt again. Then he turned to survey her angry, resentful face. His expressive mouth compressed. 'I will tell no more lies or half-truths to protect you. You're old enough to deal with reality. Your mother made *no* attempt to regain custody of you.'

'How could she when she didn't know where I was? My father was always on the move, and naturally she assumed I was with him!'

Santino emitted a pained sigh. 'After he learnt of his son's death, Gino gave me his permission to make contact with your mother—'

'I don't believe you!' Frankie cried feverishly.

'Your grandfather said, "Let my daughter-in-law come here and talk to us and then we will see what is best for the child." The next time I was in London I visited Della and informed her of Gino's invitation and your unhappiness. Your mother did nothing.'

'That's not true...that *can't* be true!'

'I'm sorry, but it is,' Santino asserted steadily, his veiled dark gaze meeting her appalled eyes and then skimming with cool diplomacy away again. 'Your mother had always known where you were because your father phoned her the day he took you, to tell her that he was bringing you to live with his family. Della has little maternal instinct, and by the time I caught up with her she was out partying every night with her second husband. Even when I told her that Marco was dead, she saw no reason why you shouldn't stay where you were.'

Frankie twisted her bright head sharply away from him, tears smarting below her lashes. A beautifully shaped masculine hand closed over her convulsing fingers and she tore free of his touch in a stark gesture of repudiation.

Santino released his breath in a raw hiss that sliced through the screamingly tense silence. 'In telling you the truth I chose the lesser of two evils. At the time, Gino could not bring himself to hurt you with that truth, and his reward was your resentment and bitterness. After your father died, you blamed your grandfather for keeping you in Sardinia. I could not let you return to your family still harbouring that grudge.'

Santino had unveiled the murky core of something Frankie had always secretly feared. Her young and beautiful mother had indeed just got on with her life once her daughter was gone—content, possibly even relieved to be free of the burden of childcare. And ever since Frankie had come home at sixteen that awful truth had been staring her in the face...hadn't it? Her fond hopes and expectations had never been met by the detached and uninterested parent she had foolishly idealised throughout her years away.

'Thank you for telling me,' Frankie breathed, tight-mouthed, falling back on her pride with fierce determination. 'But I should've been told the facts a long time ago.'

Santino drove on. 'That was not my decision to make.'

A distraught sob clogged up Frankie's throat. She despised and feared the very intensity of her own emotions. Yet it was a weakness she had learned to live with and conceal. Unfortunately that felt like an impossible challenge in Santino's presence. And just at that moment it seemed to her that in all her life she had never been loved...

Not by her emotionally cold mother, not by her feck-less father, who had stolen her purely in the vengeful hope of punishing his estranged wife, not by her father's family, who had had no choice but to keep her...and certainly not by Santino, who had already admitted to marrying her because she'd been on his conscience and he'd pitied her.

A tiny gulping sound escaped her compressed lips.

'Cry...it always makes you feel better,' Santino sug-gested, with the disturbing cool of a male who had suf-fered through countless impassioned sessions of weeping while she was in her volatile teen years.

'I hate you, Santino...' And she despised herself even more then, for sounding like a sulky adolescent.

'But you still look at me like a starving kid in a candy shop. That hasn't changed.'

A shaken surge of outrage swept over Frankie.

'What *has* changed,' Santino murmured with velvet-smooth emphasis, 'is that I no longer feel that I will be taking unfair advantage of an innocence which I now assume to be long gone...'

As his imperious dark head turned slightly, as if in question on that point, Frankie snarled, 'What do *you* think? Do you fondly imagine that the sight of you snog-ging the life out of that brassy blonde tart put me off sex for ever?'

Santino froze.

Frankie straightened her shoulders like a bristling cat, all danger of tears now banished. 'Yes, I expect you did think that. I suppose you think you broke my heart too...well, you didn't! I got over my crush on you in one second flat and, believe me, I didn't waste any time in finding a man who *did* want me—'

'Let's skip the gory details of your deflowering,' Santino interposed glacially.

Frankie flushed and dropped her head, ashamed of that outburst, particularly when it was all lies. Santino's rejection of her love had savaged her ego and made her extremely wary of trusting any man again. She had had boyfriends, of course she had, but physical intimacy had featured in none of those brief relationships. She had never met anyone she wanted as much as she had once wanted Santino and, quite frankly, she had been in no hurry to make herself that vulnerable again.

'Your family believe that you have been pursuing your education in the UK.'

Frankie was startled. 'You kept in touch with them?'

'Naturally. As far as they're concerned, I'm still your husband; I'm family too,' Santino extended gently.

Her husband. The designation and the awareness of the devastating choice he had forced on her earlier tensed every muscle in Frankie's body. Three weeks in Sardinia with Santino. Her brain went into stunned suspension. She swallowed hard. She just could not imagine going to bed with Santino. She could not even imagine Santino *wanting* to go to bed with her. This was, after all, the same male who had held her at arm's length and treated her like a kid sister during the six months they had lived under the same roof as man and wife.

Frankie had been tormented by the awareness that they were not properly married until the legal bond was consummated in the flesh. From the outset, Santino had slept in the bedroom next door. She hadn't been able to understand his extraordinary reluctance to do what Teresa had once sourly warned her all men were all too willing to do given the opportunity. And she had been too ashamed of her own obvious lack of attraction to share the humiliating secret of their separate sleeping arrangements with anyone else.

But in her innocence it had still not occurred to her that Santino might simply be satisfying his sexual appetite elsewhere. Her trust had been absolute. And she would never have found out that he had another woman in his life had she not decided to surprise him by showing up to visit him mid-week in Cagliari.

A neighbour had given her a lift to the railway station and she had caught the train the rest of the way. But she had been too intimidated by the bank to go in and actually ask for Santino. It had been lunchtime, and while she had hung around outside, trying to pluck up the courage to go inside, Santino had emerged, laughing and talking with a beautiful blonde woman. He hadn't even noticed Frankie and, disconcerted by the presence of his companion, Frankie had let them walk past. Then, scolding herself for her hesitation, naively assuming that he was merely chatting to a colleague, she had set out after them and followed them across the street. They had vanished into an elegant apartment block.

Intercepted by the security guard who asked her to explain her business, Frankie had watched in frustration as Santino and his companion strolled into the lift. And then she had watched in sick, disbelieving shock as their two bodies had merged and they'd kissed with the passionate impatience of lovers eager to be alone and out of sight of prying eyes. A split second before the doors had glided shut, Santino had lifted his beautiful dark head and seen Frankie. She would never forget the look of angry, guilty regret that had flashed across his savagely handsome features...

Dear heaven, she reflected now, five years older and wiser, and cringing from the memory of her own stupidity. Until that moment in the lift, she had sincerely believed that their marriage was a real one and that Santino had made a genuine commitment to her. But from the start Santino had naturally been planning on an annulment to regain his freedom. 'A child-bride stashed away in the mountains', he had called her. An embarrassing secret and, without doubt, an often exasperating and much resented responsibility...

*   *   *

Afternoon was fading into evening as they passed through the sleepy hill villages with their olive groves and vineyards enclosed by prickly pear hedges. As the mountain road climbed higher, the tree cover grew steadily more sparse. The pasture land took on a wild and desolate grandeur enlivened only by wandering sheep and the shepherds' rough brushwood pens. They finally reached the bare plateau and then slanted off the road onto the long, rough, steeply descending track which eventually led down into Sienta.

Stiff as a broom handle, Frankie stared out at the familiar sights all around her. Apple orchards and mature chestnut and oak trees ringed the village in its sheltered valley setting. Tiny terraced houses, their walls covered with vines, lined the sloping, twisting single street. Santino parked outside Gino Caparelli's home in the centre of the village and turned to look at her expectantly.

'Well, what are you waiting for?' he asked.

Frankie climbed out with the slowness of extreme reluctance. Then she saw her great-aunt Maddalena peering anxiously from the open doorway. Momentarily unsure of herself, she stilled, and then, without warning, a surge of overwhelming emotion engulfed her. Within seconds she was enfolded tearfully in the little woman's arms, crying and struggling to converse in a language which she had believed she had forgotten but which returned surprisingly easily to her lips.

'Come in…come in out of the street,' Teresa urged from behind her tiny sister. 'You will have all our neighbours watching us.'

And then her grandfather was before her, greeting her with a more formal embrace, pressing a salutation to her brow and then setting her back from him, frowning dark eyes below beetling white brows inspecting her. 'I would not have received you back into this house without your husband.' Gino Caparelli admitted he knew the truth be-

hind her long absence without apology. 'But now you
are back where you belong, by his side.'

Frankie's days of arguing with her grandfather's lofty
pronouncements were far behind her. She coloured and
said nothing, overwhelmed by the warm acceptance of
her welcome after five years of silence. Right at that
moment it felt like more than she deserved and she was
humbled by the experience.

Furthermore, she was seeing things she hadn't seen in
her teens, when her every thought had been exclusively
centred on Santino and escape from Sienta. She saw the
suspicious brightness and satisfaction in the older man's
eyes and then the hurt look of rejection stiffening
Teresa's thin face. Darting over, she wrapped her other
great-aunt in a belated and guilty hug.

'Bring Santino a glass of wine,' Teresa instructed
Maddalena with a rare smile as she detached herself
again. 'I will show Francesca round the house.'

Frankie frowned, not comprehending why that should
be necessary until she saw Santino and her grandfather
walk out to the little courtyard beyond the parlour. She
moved to the doorway, looking out in surprise at the
table and chairs and the decorative climbing plants
which now beautified the once unlovely space reserved
for housing Gino's fierce old sheepdog.

'When the Festrinis sold up next door, your grandfather bought their house and joined it to ours,' Teresa
announced with pride. 'We have four bedrooms now.'

'But where on earth did Nonno get the money to do
that?' Frankie prompted in astonishment.

'Gino manages all Santino's land round the village
and we look after your house,' Maddalena chipped in
cheerfully. 'We live very comfortably now.'

In a daze, Frankie let herself be carried through to the
enlarged kitchen, with its smart new stove, and on up
the stairs to inspect the pristine little bathroom which
was clearly Teresa's pride and joy. The tour then took

in the bedrooms, all of which were small and very simply furnished.

'This is where you and Santino will sleep tonight,' Maddalena informed her shyly, opening a door on a room mostly filled with a bed.

Prodded over the threshold to admire the pretty flower arrangement on the windowsill and the fresh white cotton spread on an old-fashioned wrought-iron bed that was definitely no more than four feet wide, Frankie found it a challenge to come up with the proper appreciative comments. The prospect of sharing that undersized bed with Santino deprived Frankie of all composure and strangled her usually ready tongue.

'You blush like a bride,' Teresa remarked with a wry shake of her head. 'And so you should. Isn't it time you gave that husband of yours a son?'

'Santino wanted Francesca to finish her education,' Maddalena reminded her sister gently. 'Gino thinks Santino's family must all be very educated people.'

Inwardly Francesca shrank, thinking of her humble quota of three GCSEs, until she appreciated that her lack of impressive academic qualifications scarcely mattered, for she would never meet the Vitale family in Rome. In three weeks' time, possibly even sooner, she would fly back to London and she would never see Santino again. She could not comprehend why that fact should suddenly fill her with the most peculiar sense of panic.

'When Francesca went to school here, her only interest was Santino. Had he written? Was there a letter for her...a parcel? When would he be visiting again?' Teresa was recalling with unconcealed disapproval. 'And when Santino *was* visiting with his uncle you needed eyes in the back of your head to watch her or she'd be wandering round alone with him like a shameless hussy. Oh, the gossip you gave our neighbours, Francesca! We were very lucky that Santino took you...

What other man would have after all the talk there had been?'

Frankie's face burned hotter than ever. Suddenly she was all of fourteen again, being sat down in a corner by an outraged Teresa and lectured about how improper it was for her to still chase after Santino now that she was growing up.

'They're safely married now,' Maddalena piped up soothingly.

Safe, Frankie thought sickly. There had been nothing safe about a marriage forced on a reluctant bridegroom.

Downstairs again, she was drawn into preparations for an elaborate evening meal. The men stayed out in the courtyard drinking aged Nero wine. By then it had sunk in on her that her great-aunts believed that Santino had followed her back to the UK five years ago and healed the breach between them. They thought she had been living in London with her mother solely so that she could complete her education. But then Santino had believed that too, Frankie reminded herself uncomfortably.

And, thanks to *his* generosity and support, her family had prospered as never before. That acknowledgement shamed Frankie. Santino hadn't even sold the farmhouse. He had persuaded her grandfather that his services were needed as a farm manager while his sisters acted as caretakers for the house. Without hurting their pride by offering direct financial help, Santino had given her once desperately poor family the opportunity to improve their lot in life.

From the doorway she found herself watching Santino with compulsive intensity. His luxuriant black hair gleamed in the sunshine. His chiselled profile was hard and hawkish and there was a certain restive edge to his lounging stance by the courtyard wall. Spectacular, sexy, all male. Her *husband*…?

His dark, imperious head turned, brilliant eyes narrowing and closing in on her like piercing golden arrows.

Shock shrilled through Frankie. It was like being thrown on an electric fence. Jolted, her breath caught in her throat. Helplessly she stared back at him. It was Santino who broke that connection first. With a casual word to her grandfather, he straightened and strode forward.

'I'll get your case out of the car,' he murmured huskily.

Frankie's fingers knotted together. 'Can't we go back to the farmhouse for the night?' she whispered urgently.

'And refuse your family's hospitality?' Santino surveyed her hot face and evasive eyes. He laughed softly, as if he understood exactly what was going through her mind. 'I think you know very well that that is out of the question.'

'Santino, *please*—'

He lifted a lean brown hand and let his fingertips trace the taut angle of her delicate jawbone in a fleeting gesture that made her skin tighten and her tense body jerk. 'I'll get your case,' he repeated softly, and walked away again.

Teresa planted a tablecloth and a basket of cutlery into Frankie's dazed hold and shooed her out into the courtyard.

'You have a strong man there,' Gino Caparelli mused, openly amused dark eyes resting on Frankie's tense and flushed profile. 'A strong man for a strong woman makes a good marriage.'

Her wide, full mouth tightened. 'Possibly.'

'You have learnt self-discipline. But then Santino would not tolerate tantrums.'

Frankie's lips compressed even more. When Santino made his mind up about something, he was as unyielding as bars of solid steel. She had come up against that side of Santino the first month they were married, when she had announced that she wanted to spend weekdays in Cagliari with him and he had asserted that he preferred her to stay in Sienta, close to her family. And nothing, not tears, not arguments, not sulks, not even pleas, had moved Santino one inch.

'You don't behave like a married couple of more than five years' standing,' Gino commented with an unexpected chuckle. 'That tale may content my sisters, who have never left this village in their lives...but don't worry, I am so relieved to see you with your husband again that I shall content myself with it too.'

Startled, Frankie had stilled in the act of spreading the tablecloth. Glancing up, she encountered her grandfather's alarmingly shrewd gaze. 'I—'

'You are Santino's responsibility now, and Santino could always manage you very well. With cunning, not a big stick.' Gino nodded to himself with unconcealed satisfaction and pride. 'What a match I made for you, Francesca...I saw his potential as a husband before he saw it himself!'

No truer word had her grandfather ever spoken. Frankie tried not to wince. Five and a half years ago Santino had been entrapped as much by Gino's expectations and her dependency on him as by his own sense of honour. And that same trait had made Santino assume responsibility not only for her security but for that of her Sard relatives as well. Facing up to those hard facts and setting them beside her mother's greedy self-interest, Frankie felt as though she was facing a debt that she could never repay.

'Of course I'm going to help to clear up,' Frankie protested a second time, an edge of desperation roughening her voice.

Piling up dishes with speedy efficiency, Teresa waved her hands in irritation. 'What is the matter with you? You always liked to cook, but when did you ever like cleaning up? Bring your husband more wine...attend to *his* needs,' she urged in reproof.

The candles were burning low on the table outside

and the shadows had drawn in. Tight-mouthed, Frankie hovered with the wine bottle. Santino lounged back, listening to Gino talk but contemplating Frankie with hooded but mercilessly intent dark golden eyes. With a lean hand he covered his wine glass when she would've reached for it.

'You look tired. Go to bed, *cara*. I'll be up soon,' Santino murmured with the most incredible casualness, his deep, dark drawl as smooth as oiled silk.

Frankie set down the bottle and brushed her perspiring palms down over her hips. She went into reluctant retreat, tracked every step of the way by Santino's predatory gaze. He tipped his arrogant dark head back and a dangerous smile of a very masculine tenor slanted his sensual mouth. Her heart jumped as though he had squeezed it and her hands clenched into furious fists of frustration by her side.

Five minutes in that bedroom upstairs and Frankie was convinced that she was looking at the smallest bed for two people she had ever seen in her life. It would barely take Santino, never mind her! Indeed, avoiding Santino in that bed would be an absolute impossibility. She pictured the sheer, frivolous nightwear in her case and almost curled up and died on the spot. Beautiful lingerie was her one secret extravagance, but she recoiled from the prospect of surprising Santino with an inviting display of scantily clad female flesh.

Creeping down the narrow passage into Teresa's bedroom, she extracted a voluminous high-necked cotton nightdress from the corner closet. Only the most ruthlessly determined and lustful male would try to make it past all those billowing folds in a four-foot-wide bed and with the equivalent of in-laws sleeping in the rooms on either side of them. Hugging that comforting conviction to herself, Frankie finally climbed into bed.

About half an hour later, the door opened and the bedside lamp went on. She heard Santino unzip his overnight bag. She breathed in deeply. She opened her eyes just in time to see Santino peel off his shirt. Taut as a bowstring, she studied the long golden sweep of his back, watched the ripple of tightly corded muscles as he stretched. Leaving the door ajar, he strolled barefoot across the passage into the bathroom, and only when she heard the running of water and realised that he was intending to have a bath did she breathe again.

The minutes ticked away, each of them like a saw cutting at her fast-fraying nerves. Frankie lay there getting madder and madder, responding to her own tension with growing rage. Finally the bathroom door opened again. Santino strolled back in and leant lithely against the bedroom door to close it. Frankie studied him like a bristling cat surveying a fully grown tiger invading her patch. Bare-chested, with the button on the waistband of his close-fitting jeans carelessly undone, he lounged there as if he didn't have a care in the world, long straight legs braced slightly apart.

Her mouth ran dry.

CHAPTER FIVE

'WELL, well, well, at least you're not still pretending to be asleep,' Santino commented silkily. 'Perhaps you are at long last beginning to feel just a little *married*?'

'Like heck I am!' With the greatest difficulty, Frankie dragged her attention from the intimidating breadth of his chest and the intensely masculine triangle of rough dark curls hazing his powerful pectoral muscles.

'By dawn I assure you that you will no longer be in any doubt that you belong to me.'

At that assurance, Frankie bridled in outrage. 'I do not belong to you!'

Santino sent her a winging smile that was a shockingly cold threat. 'For the next three weeks, you *do*.'

Something deep down inside Frankie shrivelled up under that chill. That distance, that detachment had been concealed in the presence of her family. Now it sprang out at her from his diamond-hard and incisive scrutiny.

'When you look at me like that, you scare me,' she muttered, and then would've done anything to retrieve that craven admission.

'You're a beautiful woman and I want to make love to you. That has nothing to do with either emotion or temper,' Santino asserted with devastating cool, and ran down the zip on his jeans.

Far from reassured, Frankie sat up with the abruptness of a puppet having her strings jerked. 'Santino…'

Santino slid out of his jeans in one fluid motion and stood there, quite unconcerned, in a pair of black briefs which did spectacularly little to conceal the overt differences between the male and female anatomy.

Hot colour flamed in Frankie's cheeks and she hurriedly averted her attention to the bedspread instead. 'Santino...*no*!' she whispered frantically.

'Why are you whispering?' he demanded, and with an undeniable lurch of dismay she saw the briefs hit the floor.

'Please, whisper back,' she begged, in an agony of embarrassment at the thought of her family hearing him.

The sheet was remorselessly wrenched from her frantically tight hold. 'I wasn't planning to do much more talking,' Santino confessed as he slid into bed with her.

'Not here...not tonight, *please*,' Frankie pleaded from the furthest edge of the mattress.

It wasn't far enough. Santino reached up with two frighteningly powerful hands and simply tumbled her down on top of him. She landed with a strangled gasp and found herself mercilessly pinned to his uncompromisingly hard male physique, startled eyes on a direct collision course with his questioning scrutiny.

'What the hell is this all about?' he enquired grimly. 'If you think you can default on an agreement with a Vitale, you are very much mistaken. What I said earlier I *meant*. What I paid for I fully intend to enjoy, however briefly.'

'But perhaps you're not thinking very clearly right now,' Frankie suggested in breathless dismay as the all-pervasive masculine heat of his naked body began to penetrate even that impregnable nightdress. 'You're still very angry with me...and you don't want to do something you might regret—'

'I want to make love to my wife, Francesca...not commit some violent criminal act,' Santino incised with considerable irony.

'If you wait until tomorrow night, I'll do anything you want!' Frankie gabbled the wildly impulsive promise in desperation.

Frowning, Santino surveyed her through the veil of

his lush black lashes. 'How many glasses of wine did you have over dinner?'

'I…I…*oh!*' Frankie gasped as he rolled her off him again, tumbled her back onto the mattress and pinned one long thigh over her trembling lower limbs.

'*Madre di Dio*…what are you wearing?' Santino enquired with incredulous volume, registering the full effect of the garment for the first time.

Frankie visibly shrank. Disorientatingly, Santino uttered a harsh laugh. He wound one hand into her tousled mane of multicoloured hair and murmured with a cynical twist of his beautifully shaped mouth, 'I wonder who first told you that what is hidden is infinitely more tantalising to most men?'

Frankie's teeth ground together. Her green eyes flashed bright with temper and disdain. 'Right…you want what you paid for…just go ahead and get it over with!' she urged with supreme scorn. 'But don't expect me to join in or pretend I like it!'

Gleaming golden eyes settled on her and flamed with slow-burning satisfaction. 'I *love* to be challenged.'

Since that had not been quite the response Frankie had foreseen, her soft mouth dropped open.

'I'll make you beg me to take you,' Santino promised.

'No…no, you won't,' Frankie mumbled in what sounded even to her own ears a very small, seriously rattled voice.

'You *always* wanted me,' Santino countered with drawling, deeply disturbing assurance. 'I could seduce you with both hands tied behind my back.'

'No…no,' she said fearfully, registering too late that that was what she was truly afraid of. Not Santino, not even the act of sex itself, but the infinitely worse threat that he might have the power to make her lose control over her own body.

'You're shaking like a leaf,' Santino whispered, when

suddenly she wanted him to shout because whispering sounded far, far too intimate.

'I'm not—'

'It's anticipation,' Santino muttered thickly. 'I know it is—'

'It's *not*!'

'Once you could burn up all the oxygen in the room just looking at me. That kind of animal attraction doesn't fade without fulfilment—'

'I grew out of it!'

His ebony brows pleating, his long, lithe body tautening, Santino studied her with sudden flaring intensity. 'Is it possible that the sight of me snogging the life out of that blonde *did* turn you off men?'

'You have the most incredible ego!' Frankie practically spat at him.

'Then there isn't the remotest possibility that you could still be a virgin?' Santino prompted tautly.

'What do you think?' Frankie snarled, at her aggressive and defensive best when it came to falling back on pride for strength. 'Do you also cherish fond hopes about Santa Claus and the Tooth Fairy?'

At her stinging sarcasm, a tiny muscle jerked at the corner of Santino's now fiercely compressed lips. '*Sì*…in this day and age you have every reason to greet such a question with incredulity.'

Over-emotional tears smarting behind her eyes, Frankie jerked her head away and blinked rapidly. She had read that it was often difficult for men to know whether or not a woman was experienced. She prayed that that was true. She could not *bear* Santino to know that she was still such an innocent! Admitting that truth would be horribly humiliating because he would instantly grasp just how deeply he had wounded her self-image with his indifference five years earlier.

Shifting, Santino lowered his dark head, his breath mingling with hers. The clean warn scent of him enveloped her. Her own breath shortened, a nervous tremor racking her.

'You're ridiculously tense…'

'What did you expect?' Frankie flared accusingly. 'This is like waiting to be attacked!'

Santino stiffened and then disconcerted her entirely by bursting out laughing. 'Is it really? And you want me to…what was that wonderful phrase?…*sì*, "just get it over with"?'

'What's so funny about that?'

With a wolfish smile that challenged, Santino gathered her to him with dauntingly sure hands and pushed her bright hair back from her cheekbones. Drawn into the raw heat of him, Frankie shivered violently. He dipped his head and, instead of directing his attention to the rigidly uninviting line of her mutinously closed mouth, he pressed his lips to the tiny pulse beating out her wild tension in the hollow of her collarbone. Frankie jerked in complete shock, bereft of breath and if possible even more alarmed by that unexpected opening move.

'You will experience only pleasure in my arms. I promise you that. In fact it is a matter of honour that you should relish sharing a bed with me.' Playing the tip of his tongue erotically across the excruciatingly tender skin of her throat, Santino sent her pulses leaping into sensual disarray. 'Open your mouth,' he urged, glittering eyes like scorching shards of pure gold.

Frankie trembled, unyielding as marble, but he brushed her mouth with his and then somehow—and later she genuinely couldn't understand how—her lips softly parted. And without the slightest warning at all Santino was kissing her with slow, deep, shattering intimacy. Her mind was just as suddenly an astonishing blank; her heart pounded in mad excitement with every rawly intrusive thrust of his tongue. What she had never counted on, and what her treacherous body had never before encountered, was that amount of sheer seductive pleasure. It was the pleasure which bowled her over and overwhelmed her.

'San—tino…' she mumbled, coming up desperately for air.

'Nothing but pleasure,' Santino promised in growling repetition.

A hot, melting sensation had begun deep down inside Frankie. Before she knew what was happening to her she was giving back kiss for kiss with frantic, driven urgency.

'You're very passionate,' Santino muttered with hoarse satisfaction, curving a firm hand over the thrust of one full breast and unerringly locating the swollen tender nipple beneath the cotton.

Involuntarily Frankie's spine arched, and a soundless gasp was torn from her as he gently, deftly used that barrier that she had naively hoped would frustrate him to excite her beyond all bearing. As, with his guidance, the coarse grain of the fabric massaged and tormented those achingly sensitive buds, Frankie started burning all over and found it quite impossible to stay still.

An arrow of piercing heat twisted between her restive thighs. He lowered his mouth to the straining peaks and still the screening material failed to lessen the depth of her response. Indeed her whole body jackknifed under that fresh onslaught. A strangled moan was wrenched from her and instantly he covered her mouth with his again, silencing her.

'Hush, *cara*…' Santino instructed in his deep, dark drawl as he ran an exploring and incredibly arousing hand down the quivering length of one securely cotton-shrouded thigh. 'I haven't even begun yet.'

But, whether he had begun or not, Frankie's sensation-starved body was already out of her control, and seething with a feverish, needy passion utterly outside her experience. She clutched at his shoulders with straining fingers, striving to find his mouth again for herself. And then, still quite tormentingly indifferent to the shielding thickness of the nightdress, which was now driving her to the heights of screaming frustration because she wanted so badly to feel her skin naked against his, Santino discovered the most sensitive place of all with an impossibly gentle hand.

A tortured moan of intolerable hunger escaped Frankie. 'Take the wretched thing off,' she pleaded.

'Shush,' Santino soothed, while doing everything possible to ensure that the only way she could keep quiet was either to bite him or bite the pillow. 'I know what I'm doing.'

It was more than Frankie did. Twisting and turning against him, out of her mind with excitement, her entire body was clenched unbearably tight by the burning hunger he had ignited with his touch. Lost and driven without her own volition to a shattering peak of hunger, an explosion of ecstatic pleasure burst without warning inside her, plunging her into wave after wave of drugging sensual delight. At the same moment Santino crushed her under him and sealed his mouth to hers to swallow every gasping cry she made.

When he freed her and she was able to breathe again, Frankie was in so much shock she was a shadow of her usual aggressive self, limp with the satiation of physical gratification and simultaneously devastated by the experience.

In the thundering silence, Santino scanned her shaken face and dazed eyes with a disturbingly shrewd look of satisfaction. 'Now *that* was definitely a first for you.'

Assailed by the most outraged sense of seething mortification, Frankie thrust him away from her with wild and frantic hands. Turning her back on him, she curled up as warily stiff as a hedgehog ready to repel attack. The light went out. She lay there, boiling alive with shame at the awareness that Santino had watched her lose all control while he caressed her wanton, hatefully responsive body. And he hadn't even had to take her nightdress off...though she had actually begged him to remove it, she recalled strickenly, absolutely horrified by her own behaviour.

A long arm plucked her off the very edge of the mattress and drew her remorselessly back into all too physical contact. Frankie went rigid but Santino ignored the fact. Flipping her over, indifferent to the imprisoning folds of the nightdress entrapping her, he sealed her into relentless connection with his long, lithe body. In the moonlight, her eyes flew wide. Against her stomach she felt the shocking proof that he was still very aroused. He had given her the pleasure he had promised but had as yet taken none for himself.

'You said if I waited until tomorrow night you'd do anything I want,' Santino reminded her, with terrifying timing and truly devastating effect. 'A provocative offer...and for me? Pure erotic temptation. So for what remains of tonight I will practise patience and self-restraint...'

Whipped back into life by that tigerish taunting purr, Frankie very nearly exploded with temper. And then she bit her lower lip so hard she hurt herself, but contrived to practise some much needed restraint of her own while she continued to squirm at the memory of him cutting off her whimpers and moans of excitement with kisses.

'Unless you've changed your mind...?'

'No...no, I haven't,' Frankie mumbled, wondering if she had been temporarily insane to say such a thing to a virile male as experienced as Santino. Precisely what would he want her to do? Hurriedly shutting that enervating thought back out again, Frankie breathed in slowly and carefully to calm herself. Tomorrow night felt like a long way away.

Frankie stared into the little mirror propped on top of the chest of drawers and hated what she saw. A woman

who had let herself down a bucketful. If she had reacted
with revulsion when he'd touched her, Santino would
not have persisted. But then what might he have done?
Gone back to his original plan to evict Della and prosecute her for fraud? Frankie shivered. No matter how
badly Della had behaved, Frankie couldn't bear to think
of her mother being humiliated to that extent.

And Frankie was painfully aware that she had betrayed herself to Santino. He had recognised her hunger
and chosen a punishment calculated to decimate her
pride. And why shouldn't he have? she conceded, with
new and bitter acceptance of the situation she had im-
pulsively put herself in. After all, she had stood herself
beside Della and had deliberately taken on the guise of
a mercenary little confidence trickster.

Now she was reaping the benefit of Santino's angry
and vengeful contempt. Santino who knew her so much
better than anyone else alive; Santino who knew exactly
how much her pride meant to her…Santino who would
be quite capable of tearing her to tiny emotional shreds
in the space of three weeks. For she didn't know Santino,
not as he was now.

She was so vulnerable where he was concerned. And
it wasn't just that she still found him wildly attractive.
Ninety-nine out of a hundred women would take one
look at Santino and go weak at the knees. He had spectacular looks and an electrifying aura of sensual dominance. But Frankie was also threatened by infinitely
more subtle and dangerous promptings. For Frankie,
Santino had just always been so special. So terrifyingly,
hopelessly *special*…

The door opened without warning. In the act of plait-
ing her hair, Frankie flinched. Santino stilled in the doorway, lean, mean and magnificent in a black shirt and
black close-fitting moleskin jeans. 'Breakfast is almost
ready.'

As she collided reluctantly with lustrous dark golden

eyes, her entire face burned. It seemed to her that there was a new knowledge in his steady gaze, a sardonic male savouring of her abandonment in his arms only hours earlier. Turning back to the mirror, she said coldly, 'I'll be down in a minute.'

'Don't you have a skirt in that case?' Santino enquired drily.

Frankie skimmed an irritably self-conscious hand down over her navy cotton trousers. 'I don't like skirts.'

'I do…and what I like you have to like for the next three weeks.' Santino delivered the reminder without remorse.

'You think I'm going to turn into some sort of combination sex-slave and dress-up doll?' Frankie enquired, tight-mouthed, breasts swelling with chagrin as she sucked in a deep restraining breath. 'Well, you've got the wrong woman—'

'I don't think so.' Santino appeared behind her in the mirror and she tensed in surprise. He loosened the plait with ruthless cool and planted the brush back into her nerveless fingers. 'You can't suppress that passion in the same way that you strive to conceal that glorious hair. I won't let you.'

Frankie trembled with rage. 'Don't tell me what I can't do—'

'So find out the hard way what happens when you rebel. That seems to be the only way you ever learn,' Santino said flatly. 'Just as you learned last night that the family you spent all those years trying to escape actually love you.'

Choked up by that reminder, temper cruelly squashed by it, Frankie froze. 'I *know*,' she muttered guiltily.

'And when I fade back out of their lives again you will stay in touch,' Santino told her grimly. 'You can blame me for breaking up our marriage and tell them you got the farm in the divorce. They have about as much grasp of the extent of my wealth as you once had.'

'But they're fond of you too...' Frankie heard herself protest shakily.

'I still won't be back,' Santino drawled with flat conviction. 'I think that in your absence I have done everything that could reasonably be expected of me, but my responsibility here is now drawing to an end.'

'For a bigshot like you, it must've been a real drag to come visiting out in the boonies!' Frankie flung, in a distress she couldn't even understand.

Santino's lean hands came down on her taut shoulders to spin her round. Ice-cool dark eyes scanned her over-bright gaze and the sudden intense confusion etched there. 'Keep those emotions under control,' he advised harshly. 'I may want that beautiful body but that's the only interest I have now. At the end of this little interlude, I have every intention of walking away.'

Frankie gulped. 'You think that's not what I want too?'

'I think you're programmed to attach yourself to the wrong people, and I really don't want to pay a second time. This is just the settlement of a long-overdue debt, Francesca. Try to keep that in mind.'

Frankie stared into the mirror long after Santino had gone, registered the stricken look in her eyes and closed them because she could not bear to see what he might have seen.

CHAPTER SIX

AFTER lunch, Santino drove Frankie out to the farmhouse. She had spent the entire morning with Teresa and Maddalena, making ceremonial calls on several neighbours. In a village where most of the young people left as soon as they were old enough to seek work there was nothing unusual about the length of her absence, and warm hospitality had greeted her everywhere.

However, thunderous tension-filled silence reigned between Santino and Frankie as he turned the Landcruiser up the lane to the dwelling which had once so briefly been their home. Everywhere Frankie looked she was stabbed to the heart by memories with a very raw edge. Her first glimpse of the house with its weathered stone walls and red-tiled roof simply choked her up. Determined as she was not to betray a single emotional reaction, her facial muscles locked defensively tight as she climbed out of the car.

'What happened to my hens?' she enquired stiffly.

'I should imagine someone finally ate them.'

Careful not to look at him, Frankie breathed tightly, 'Angela?'

'Went to that great goat heaven in the sky.'

'Milly and her calf?' Frankie pressed even more tautly.

'Sold.'

Frankie was now rigid. 'Topsy…and Pudding?' she prompted, half an octave higher. 'They've gone too, haven't they?'

'Yes.'

Unable to contain herself any longer, Frankie rounded

on Santino. 'So what did you *do* with my cats?' she demanded rawly. 'Did you eat them, sell them or bury them?'

Brilliant dark eyes rested on her fearful, accusing face. 'I took them back to Rome with me.'

'O-oh…' Reddening with sudden embarrassment and surprise, Frankie folded her arms jerkily and turned away again.

Trembling, she preceded him into the house and walked straight into the cosy, low-ceilinged lounge with its comfortable twin sofas. From the rear window she looked out in dismay at the garden which she had created five years earlier. It had been swallowed up by brambles and scrub. So what? she asked herself. This is not my home any more; this was *never* really my home. None of these changes matter to me in the slightest, the inner voice insisted. But, in spite of that sensible voice, pained regret and a strong feeling of resentful loss still washed over Frankie.

She had adored this house only one iota less than she had once adored Santino. After the cramped and basic confines of her grandfather's home, this spacious house had seemed like a palace. No sixteen-year-old bride had ever been more deliriously happy with her lot. All that bright, innocent hope and unquestioning trust… She felt such a fool looking back on it now, particularly when she thought of the *castello*…

Maids and antique furniture and fancy bathrooms. That was Santino's true milieu. Yet, five years ago, he had valiantly roughed it every weekend in what to him had to have been the equivalent of a hovel. In keeping with Sard tradition he had bought the house and furnished it before the wedding. He had brought her paint cards, picked her favourite colours, become the first person in Sienta to pay someone else to decorate—an extravagance which had had Gino Caparelli shaking his head with appalled incredulity. But in every other way

Santino had done exactly what was expected of a Sard bridegroom.

'I hate you, Santino,' Frankie breathed unevenly, swallowing the great lump threatening her throat. 'If I played house, I played house because *you* encouraged me to do that!'

'What else was I supposed to do with you?' Santino responded to that accusation levelly. 'As you were then, you couldn't have handled my family, and they couldn't have handled you.'

Flinching from that blunt stating of fact, Frankie nonetheless spun straight back to him. 'I don't think there was *ever* any question of my meeting your family,' she challenged in condemnation.

Santino elevated a smooth ebony brow, his vibrantly handsome features impassive. 'It's immaterial now.'

The unspoken reminder of how much time had passed since then silenced her. She had sounded like a woman scorned, she thought in horror. Bitter, accusing. All over what? A marriage that had never been a normal marriage? A husband who had never been a real husband and who had, understandably, at the age of twenty-four, found celibacy too much of a challenge?

Twisting away, dismally conscious of how close her turbulent emotions were to the surface and how great would be the self-betrayal if she voiced those raw feelings, Frankie stalked out of the room and started up the narrow staircase. On the landing, however, her deep sense of injustice overcame her. 'You should've just come to see me in London...you should *never* have dragged me back here!'

She flashed into what should have been and never had been the marital bedroom. Here she had slept alone. At the foot of the bed rested the carved dower chest presented to her by her great-aunts on her wedding day, filled to the brim with exquisite embroidered linen. Teresa and Maddalena had given the chest with such pride and pleasure. Neither of them had ever married, and no Sard woman of their generation celebrated spinsterhood.

She stood at the low window, staring sightlessly out. Santino evoked a dangerously explosive mix of hatred and fierce longing inside her. The hatred she wanted to nourish, but the strength of that fierce longing filled her with fear. Dear heaven, Santino was already tearing her apart. He was forcing her to relive so much that she had deliberately buried.

'Francesca...' Santino murmured from the doorway.

Her hands closed convulsively in on themselves. 'I was so happy here,' she whispered, and then, instantly regretting that lowering admission—for who wanted to admit to having been happy living in a pathetic dreamworld?—she added curtly, 'You should have told me the truth about our marriage right from the start.'

'I didn't think you were strong enough to take it,' Santino countered with devastating frankness. 'You had too much invested in our relationship.'

Frankie's restive fingers coiled into tight fists. 'That's not true!' She flipped round to face him. 'I've had my share of hard knocks in life, but none of them has ever sent me to the wall!'

Santino surveyed her with steady, dark-as-night eyes, as if he knew that she was lying, as if he *knew* that he had cruelly ripped her heart out that day in Cagliari and almost destroyed her. 'You were completely dependent on me and extremely vulnerable. You had the body and the emotions of an adult without the maturity or the experience...' Unusually, Santino hesitated, his deep, dark drawl roughening as he breathed, 'After five years of living in such isolation your knowledge of the world barely went beyond the boundaries of this village.'

Frankie paled and veiled her expressive eyes, appalled by an assessment she could not protest at. Too well did

she recall the frightening disorientation she had endured
when she had returned to London.

'If you hadn't caught the train to Cagliari that day,
you would eventually have agreed to continue your education in Florence,' Santino asserted with conviction. 'I
would have been able to watch over you there. You
would have outgrown your infatuation with me and
found yourself becoming more interested in boys in your
own age group.'

Frankie bit back a sarcastic shout of disbelief but
could not resist prompting, 'And if I *hadn't*...what
would you have done then?'

Santino shifted a powerful shoulder in an infinitesimal
shrug, brilliant eyes screened by thick black lashes. 'I
would have coped with the situation. I was very fond of
you.'

Fond. A shudder of revulsion and mortification rip-
pled through her taut length. What a lukewarm, milky
nothing word, she reflected fiercely.

'But, regardless of that, we couldn't have gone on
living as we were. I didn't want to risk ending up in bed
with you—'

'Oh, I don't think there was ever much risk of that!'
Francesca hissed with the sharpness of unforgotten pain
as she tried to brush past him.

Santino snaked out a lean brown hand and closed it
round her slender forearm to force her to still. His dark
eyes shimmered with flaring gold anger as he gazed
down at her. 'You were as wild as a gypsy. Incredibly
beautiful and stunningly sexy. You didn't even appear
to be aware of your sexual power, but it *was* there and
it kept me awake every night I ever spent in this house
with you,' Santino informed her rawly. 'You were a
temptation that tormented me every day of our marriage.'

Stunned into paralysis by that staggering admission,

Frankie stared up at him, green eyes wide with disbelief, even her breathing suspended.

'I walked a tightrope with you,' Santino recalled grimly, a line of dark colour accentuating the spectacular slant of his hard cheekbones. 'I knew that if I succumbed I'd plunge us both into an impossible relationship. I deserved a medal for staying out of the marital bed...most particularly when you began reminding me at every opportunity that you *were* my wife!'

Oxygen re-inflated Frankie's lungs as she sucked in a shuddering breath. Shock still rolled over her in heady waves, but a surge of deep and abiding anger followed in its wake. Wrenching herself violently free, she raced down the stairs and out of the back door into the fresh air.

All that time he had wanted her; all that time and she had never once suspected. A jagged laugh was wrenched from her. She had loved him *so* much. She had loved Santino with an intensity that had been unashamed and fearless. Unable to imagine a future without him, she hadn't understood how much damage loving like that could do until it was too late to protect herself. But all along Santino had known...

In spite of the heat, her skin chilled. 'You had too much invested in our relationship.' With those bloodless words of detachment, Santino had acknowledged the reality that she had belonged to him body and soul. So he had been physically attracted to her; so he had been tempted by the body she had been so pitifully willing to offer...it meant so little, she conceded painfully. It was like coming in last of all in a race she had once hoped to win.

For Santino had withstood sexual temptation with colossal cool and self-discipline. They had cracked the mould when they made Santino. Lust had warred with intellect...and intellect had naturally won. A strong and shrewd instinct for self-preservation had kept Santino out of the marital bed. He had known that he'd have a hell of a job getting rid of her if he slept with her.

A lean hand came down on her shoulder. Santino turned her round, gleaming dark golden eyes scanning her flushed and expressive face. 'You are still very intense,' he murmured thoughtfully. 'Still remarkably sensitive to the past. And yet why should I be surprised by that? The Sard blood in your veins fuelled your desire for revenge. I hurt you. And you retaliated in the only way you could. You chose to lie and cheat and steal from me.'

Paling, Frankie muttered, 'I…I—'

Santino's strong dark features were hard and unyielding. 'I've already explained why I behaved as I did then. And yet still you show no shame. That explanation should've been unnecessary. No decent man would've bedded an infatuated teenager!'

Frankie's temper sparked. 'No decent man would've broken his marriage vows either! You were unfaithful. Where's your shame, Santino?' she shot at him, unable to silence that angry demand.

Disconcerted by that spontaneous counter-attack, Santino breathed slowly, '*My* shame?'

'I was your wife. Age doesn't come into it. You married me. You made promises to me. You *broke* them!' Frankie enumerated with raw bite. 'Am I supposed to be grateful because you stooped to marrying me in the first place? Well, I'm not grateful. In fact, I blame you for that most of all. You gave me expectations I would never have had otherwise. You allowed me to believe that I had rights when I had no rights! That was cruel and unfair and very short-sighted. How was I supposed to recover from my infatuation when I thought of you as my husband?'

Her outspoken censure provoked an incredulous flash in Santino's hard scrutiny. Satisfaction filled Frankie. He was a self-righteous rat, blind to his own errors of judgement. Marrying her hadn't been a kindness or a damage-limitation exercise. It had been sheer madness to encourage her love and dependency with a wedding ring.

She lifted her fiery head high, the burden of the past lightening, for she had finally got to put her own point of view and pride had been redeemed. Taking advantage of Santino's charged stillness, she crossed with a sinuous twist of her hips through a gap in the prickly pear boundary to the rough pasture land beyond. 'I'm going for a walk,' she announced.

A long while later, she sank down on a sun-baked rock to stare down at the farmhouse, stubborn resolution etched in every line of her lovely face. At last she felt free of that shadowy teenage self who had been relentlessly haunting her. And she had rediscovered the fighting backbone she needed to deal with Santino. Once he had put her through an emotional wringer, but she would never give him the power to hurt her like that again.

Matt—whom she absolutely had to phone, she reminded herself in exasperation—well, Matt had suggested that this trip might be therapeutic. And, astonishingly, he had hit a bull's-eye with that forecast. It *was* time to move on. It *was* time she got Santino out of her system. And, since she had always been wildly attracted to Santino, wasn't it ridiculously old-fashioned to be ashamed of the fact? Everything that drew her to Santino had to have its roots in that physical hunger.

They would have a passionate affair and nobody would ever know about it. Then they would part and, most importantly, she would be *over* him. Santino's indifference had once smashed her ego. That was why she had never been able to put him behind her, where he belonged. That was undoubtedly why she was still so strongly drawn to him. Human nature was perverse. Didn't people always want what they thought they couldn't have?

When curiosity was satisfied, surely she would be

completely cured of this hangover from her past? Convincing herself of that cheered Frankie up immensely.

'I've started a meal. I thought you might like a drink,' Frankie said breezily as she strolled into the room across from the lounge which Santino had always used as an office.

Santino spun round in surprise from the computer, brilliant eyes reflecting the sunlight and momentarily stilling her. Smiling brightly, Frankie set the glass of wine down on the desk, struggling not to cringe at the sight of the large bridal photograph of herself that she had placed on that same desk five years earlier, and which still sat there, an embarrassing rave from the grave.

'Heavens, does nobody ever dump anything around here?' she complained, lifting the frame and treating it to a disparaging glance before she dropped it with a gentle crash down into the waste-paper bin. 'Sorry, but it's really creepy seeing stuff like that still sitting about.'

Relishing the slight frown drawing Santino's winged ebony brows together, Frankie walked back to the door, secure in the knowledge that her behaviour was disconcerting him. 'Dinner won't be ready for ages yet. I thought I should make this a special occasion,' she murmured sweetly, casting her dancing eyes down. 'What a pity you didn't lay in some champagne...'

Ten minutes later she was standing beneath the bathroom shower, deciding to wear her bathing pareu and possibly her most abbreviated top in which to dine. Santino wanted to see her in a skirt again? She was feeling generous. Santino wanted revenge? Well, Santino was in for a disappointment there. Frankie was the person planning to be empowered by the night ahead. She was going to wash that man right out of her hair and walk away, strengthened and renewed by the experience.

Ironically, Santino had greatly revived her self-image with the astonishing confession that he had found her an almost unbearable temptation at sixteen. *Before* she'd got her slight overbite corrected, *before* she'd got dress sense, *before* she'd become an independent and surely far more interesting adult woman...

So he ought to be a push-over for seduction. And she might be inexperienced but she knew all the mechanics, could hardly fail to be aware of them. The British media surfeit of articles on sensual experimentation was thrust at women from every printed page. And surely knowledge was power in the bedroom?

Downstairs in the lounge she lifted the phone and belatedly tried to ring Matt, but her business partner was out. She left a brief message on the answering machine at the apartment, explaining that so far she had been unable to reach agreement with the owner of the villas. Strictly true, not a lie, she thought ruefully.

The fridge in the kitchen was crammed with fresh food and the cupboards were fully stocked. Her greataunts had been wonderfully thorough. Frankie hummed as she baked *carta da musica* bread, checked the selection of *antipasti* appetisers and the clear soup she had already prepared and went on to make an asparagus salad, *gnocchetti alla sarda* for a main course and a pecorino-based cheesecake to be served with Sard bitter honey.

Gastronomically, Santino would be as putty in her ruthless hands. She had a second glass of wine to fortify herself. Tonight there would be none of last night's craven uncertainty. Tonight she would hold centre stage and *she* would be in control. When she had the table prepared, she called him.

Santino stilled one step inside the dining room. Brilliant dark eyes raked with infuriating impassivity over the candlelit intimacy of the beautifully set table and then lodged on Frankie, where she positively posed, the colourful pareu knotted at her slender waist and arranged to reveal a discreet stretch of one long, fabulous leg. His intent gaze roamed over her flowing mane of vibrant hair and the strappy green T-shirt which revealed rather more than it concealed of her high, full breasts.

Frankie held her breath, heartbeat crashing like warning thunder in her eardrums. Her own attention was all for him. In a dinner jacket and close-fitting black trousers, with a white dress shirt heightening the exotic effect of his black hair and golden skin, he looked alien and yet alarmingly, wonderfully spectacular. A tingle ran down her responsive spine.

'Are you planning to poison me during the first course?' Santino enquired lethally.

Frankie stiffened incredulously. 'Is that supposed to be a joke?'

'I know you're temperamental, but this scenario is unbelievable. ''Come into my parlour said the spider to the fly…'''

Feeling foolish, Frankie tilted her chin in challenge. 'Why shouldn't I amuse myself by cooking up a storm when I've got nothing better to do?'

Santino's sensual mouth slanted with unsettling sardonic amusement. 'A complete volte-face within the space of hours? Naturally I'm suspicious.'

'Just sit down and *eat*!' Frankie stalked back out to the kitchen.

She poured herself another glass of wine with an angry hand. So Santino refused to be impressed. Damn him for having the power to play his cards so close to his chest, not to mention the dismaying ability to look at her, in spite of all her efforts, as he might have looked at a stone statue.

'You could ravish a saint in that outfit,' Santino drawled with silken mockery from the doorway. 'You look gorgeous from top to toe. Happy now? But when you stood there patently expecting me to compliment you something in me refused to give you what you wanted.'

Frankie focused on him with mortified resentment. He made her sound so naive, so *obvious*. Sidestepping him, she returned to the table. 'That's because you're devious and stubborn, Santino...you always were. I used to not see that, but now I do,' she confided with driven honesty.

'So be warned,' Santino murmured chillingly. 'I have never liked games, Francesca.'

Her lashes lowered, her appetite ebbing. When she glanced up again, Santino was uncorking a dusty bottle of champagne. 'Where did that come from?'

'It was in the cellar,' he revealed. 'Waiting for just such an opportunity.'

Frankie played restively with her food and just watched him eat. Whenever she looked at him her mouth ran dry. In her mind's eye she was trying to picture them in that bed upstairs. Anxiety at the challenge she had set herself and the tingling heat of undeniable anticipation warred like mutual enemies inside her. Every time she went out to the kitchen she drank more wine. As she sank deeper into abstraction, Santino's polished attempts to make conversation earned only monosyllabic responses.

Over the dessert course, she surveyed him and breathed in an abrupt tone of discovery, 'You secretly wanted me to be a virgin, didn't you?'

Santino's superb bone structure tensed, lush black lashes narrowing on fiercely intent but uncommunicative eyes. 'Now why would you think that?'

Frankie propped her chin on the heel of one hand, knowing she had startled him almost as much as she had startled herself with that sudden suspicion. A rather malicious smile formed on her generous mouth. 'I can't explain it, but somehow I know it's the truth. You must be very disappointed.'

'Hardly.' His beautiful mouth curled as he met that

provocative smile head-on. 'I can think of no more te-
dious a start to a brief affair than the need to initiate a
nervous amateur.'

The silence stretched. Frankie had paled.

'I was just self-conscious last night,' she informed
him even more abruptly. 'Usually I'm very confident in
the bedroom.'

'Good...I'm feeling unusually shy tonight,' Santino
imparted silkily.

Involuntarily, Frankie studied him, her heart banging
frantically fast against her ribs. Those incredible mag-
netic eyes of his. She wanted to drown in them. Maybe
that was why her head was swimming and it was taking
such appalling effort to concentrate. 'Coffee?' she asked
jerkily.

Santino watched the tip of her pink tongue snake out
to moisten her dry lower lip. He tensed, and then rose
in one fluid sweep from behind the table. Deftly depriving her of her glass, he drew her up into his arms. 'Not
for me,' he breathed huskily.

A ripple of quite tormented excitement ran through
Frankie. Long fingers curved against her spine and
pressed her closer. Her pent-up breath escaped in a
shaken hiss as she registered the swollen fullness of her
breasts and the urgent sensitivity of her nipples, but the
power of those sensations was somewhat diminished by
the disorientating dizziness assailing her.

'Let's go to bed,' Santino suggested, his deep, dark
drawl fracturing to send a responsive frisson through her
trembling length.

Frankie closed her eyes to block him out and resist
the overpowering pull of his dominance. This wasn't
how she had planned it. *He* was taking control.
'No...you go up...you wait for me tonight,' she urged,
wondering why her words were slurring.

'OK.' She lifted her lashes and caught his faint frown
and then watched him stride towards the stairs.

Swaying slightly, she steadied herself on the chair-back, dismay gripping her. Rather too late she was appreciating that she had had too much to drink and far too little to eat. She was furious with herself for being so stupid. Pouring herself a cup of black coffee, she forced it down and then crept outside to breathe in great gulps of the night air in the hope of sobering herself up again.

Her head a little clearer, she nonetheless plotted a far from straight path up the stairs. She could still do it. She could, she *could*. Santino was waiting for her just the way she had planned it, so she wouldn't risk embarrassing herself with potentially clumsy attempts to undress him. And there he was in the marital bed for the very first time in his life…

At that enervating sight something akin to pure anguish seized Frankie. Santino was a gorgeous vision of raw masculine appeal against the white bedlinen. All tousled and golden and breathtakingly sexy…and she was feeling…she was suddenly feeling so horribly sick, and the room was revolving round her in the most nauseating way.

'What's the matter with you?' Santino demanded as he thrust the sheet back with startling abruptness. '*Dio*…I thought it was my imagination downstairs, but you're—'

Frankie made a most undignified dive for the bathroom across the landing. Her worst apprehensions were fully fulfilled. Afterwards she just wanted to be left alone to die, but no such mercy awaited her.

'You'll feel a lot better after you eat,' Santino asserted drily.

Unconvinced, Frankie stared down at the rather charred toast on the breakfast tray. It was safer than looking at Santino. Severe embarrassment clawed at her, for she recalled almost every awful moment of the previous night. Santino initially incredulous at the state she was in, then impatient, exasperated, but ultimately kind. And *why* had he been kind? It was bred into Santino's privileged bones to be kind towards those weaker or less able than he was. She squirmed, pride choking on a generosity which had only increased her sense of humiliation.

'Thank you,' she contrived between clenched teeth, pushing up the sliding strap of the slinky nightdress she had woken up in, shamed as only a woman could be by the knowledge that she had no recollection of donning the garment.

'There has to be a reason why you got that drunk.'

'I wasn't drunk...I was only a bit tipsy,' she countered, so desperate to escape a post mortem, she even bit into a piece of that unappetising toast while wondering if she ought to preserve it for posterity. Unless she was very much mistaken, this toast was the closest Santino had ever come to cooking.

'Are you in love with Matt Finlay?'

Frankie almost choked on the toast. 'Of course I'm not...he's just a friend!' she spluttered in frustration.

Santino contemplated her with galling cool. 'Then you over-indulged because you were nervous—'

'That's ridiculous! Why do you have to make such heavy weather out of something that was purely accidental?'

Santino's beautiful mouth clenched hard. 'Possibly because the idea of you endangering yourself with such reckless behaviour in the company of a less scrupulous male angers me. You should know better.'

'The days when I looked to you to tell me how to behave are far behind me.'

Santino dealt her a derisive glance from the doorway. 'It *shows*.'

Head lowering, cheeks burning, Frankie swallowed convulsively.

Having believed Santino had left the room, she was startled when the tray was lifted away and he sank down instead on the edge of the bed. Unprepared for that proximity, her pained eyes unguarded, she stiffened defensively as he threaded long, sure fingers through her wildly tumbled hair in a disturbingly comforting gesture.

And then, without warning, Santino smiled, one of those blinding, sudden, charismatic smiles that shook her up and made her treacherous heart race. 'That wasn't a very generous comment when you spent so much time apologising last night,' he conceded huskily.

He was so close she could smell the hot, sun-warmed scent of him, intrinsically male and powerfully familiar. Her nostrils flared, her breath catching in her throat as she raised an involuntary hand and let her fingers rest on one broad shoulder to steady herself, her gaze welded to the shimmering gold of his. She shivered as he eased her forward and bent his dark head. A warm, drugging anticipation trapped her in submissive stillness.

He kissed her very gently, his tenderness a soothing balm to her smarting sensitivities. And it made her want him even more. In fact it made her want to cling. He tasted her lips in tiny hungry forays that sent her arms snaking round him in desperation to pull him closer. Her whole body felt as if it was reaching up and out, craving what only he could give. An explosive charge of hunger burned up inside her, and when his tongue penetrated between her readily parted lips her heart lurched so violently she could barely breathe in the seething excitement that controlled her.

Santino lifted his imperious dark head and absorbed her dazed expression. His strong face impassive, he sprang lithely upright. A tiny pulse flickered at the corner of his compressed mouth but in every other way he looked utterly relaxed and in control. 'I haven't had breakfast yet,' he murmured, and strode gracefully out of the room.

Chilled by that abrupt withdrawal, Frankie flopped back against the pillows, stunned by the passion he had fired and then abandoned. Had he regretted that terrifyingly seductive instant of tenderness at the outset? No matter…he had still cut through her prickly defences as easily as a child knocking down a wobbly tower of building blocks—and, worst of all, he was well aware of the fact.

Her hands trembled as she reached for the tray again. Physical hunger, that was *all* it was, she told herself, and maybe she was more susceptible than he was in her inexperience. Only that didn't explain why she had suffered a great suffocating attack of fear and insecurity as she'd watched him detach himself from her and walk away.

She was emerging from the shower when she thought she heard the knocker sounding on the front door. Snatching up Santino's towelling robe, she pulled it on hurriedly and walked out onto the landing.

'Francesca?' Santino called softly. 'Come downstairs.'

With a frown she moved to the head of the staircase. In amazement she gazed down at Matt where he stood in the hall, equally welded to the spot by the sight of her.

'M-Matt?' she stammered in amazement.

'Yes…*Matt*,' her business partner confirmed thinly as he ran indignant eyes over her flustered and damp appearance in the oversized male garment she wore. 'Would you like to tell me what's going on here?'

CHAPTER SEVEN

THE tension in the hall was so thick it sent a shocking trickle of apprehension down Frankie's spine as she descended the stairs. Matt's fair face was flushed and he looked, to her, incomprehensibly furious and accusing. Her attention skimmed to Santino, who stood with impenetrable eyes and a curiously threatening quality of absolute stillness.

'What on earth are you doing here, Matt?' Frankie began uncertainly. 'How did you even find out where I was?'

'This was the only place left to look,' Matt returned. 'I remembered the name of this village and I knew you had family here... But why the blazes didn't you tell someone where you were going?'

'I left a message on the apartment answering machine yesterday...' Frankie continued to stare at him in astonishment for she could imagine no good reason for Matt to leave the agency and come racing over to Sardinia in search of her. 'I know I was a little tardy with that call, but what made you think you needed to fly over here to track me down?'

'Your mother—'

'My...*mother*?' Frankie interrupted incredulously.

Matt swore, only half under his breath. 'I wasn't unduly concerned about your silence until I called your mother to ask if you'd been in touch with her. The minute she realised that you were in Sardinia and that I hadn't heard from you, she went off into blasted hysterics.'

'Hysterics?' Frankie echoed in a wobbly voice, unable to imagine Della in such an emotional state.

'So naturally that panicked *me*, and when I found out that your hire car had been returned it did look very suspicious. Nobody about to go on a touring holiday dispenses with their only means of transport. It seemed like you had disappeared off the face of this earth!'

Frankie was horribly embarrassed by her own thoughtlessness. 'It honestly never occurred to me that anyone would worry...nobody ever has before—'

'You've never staged a vanishing act before. Your mother's called in the police—'

'The *police*?' Frankie blinked, appalled. 'I'm sorry...I just don't understand what's got into everybody—'

'Yes, well, personally speaking, neither do I.' Matt shot a resentful glance of unease at Santino, who had gone rigid at the reference to the police, his jawline taking on a distinctly aggressive slant. 'But you made the headlines on the television news last night. British tourist missing—'

'Oh, no...' Frankie mumbled weakly.

'Della thinks you've either been kidnapped because of your secret wealthy connections or—'

'Kidnapped?' Santino incised in an outraged growl.

'Or because of some crazy vendetta against you by that same *secret* connection,' Matt completed with considerable sarcasm, surveying Santino with naked antipathy. 'I think we can rule out both possibilities, since you appear to be on such cosy and intimate terms with your estranged husband.'

'Oh, heck, I'd better phone Mum... Matt, I'm *so* sorry... I really don't know what could've made Della carry on like this—'

'Guilt,' Santino ground out grittily.

'You should've told me you were still married. You told me everything else.' Matt glowered accusingly at

Frankie. 'Does *he* know how long you've been shacked up with me?'

'Sh-shacked up with you?' Frankie was thoroughly disconcerted by that misleading description of the terms on which they shared the same apartment.

'Yes…what kind of kinky marital relationship do you two have?' Matt sent Santino a malicious half-smile. 'I hope you appreciate that she runs around with a lot of other men too… Here today, forgets you're alive tomorrow. That's my Frankie!'

Santino lunged off the wall like a ferocious tiger suddenly provoked by a whip. 'You—!'

'*Please…!*' Frankie yelped in horror, and, grabbing Matt's arm, she yanked the smaller man hurriedly into the lounge with her, speedily slamming the door on Santino's unfamiliar and frightening aggression. 'Why are you behaving like this, Matt? What the heck's got into you?'

Matt stiffened with an angry jerk. 'I thought I *knew* you! I thought we were a pretty successful team. I even thought I would marry you…it certainly would've made good business sense.'

Frankie stiffened at that revealing admission. Seemingly her share of the agency had been her greatest attraction in Matt's eyes. 'But you never showed the slightest personal interest in me until Leigh moved out of the apartment. We were just flatmates. We led separate lives outside working hours—'

Matt wasn't listening. 'So that is Santino…your husband since you were sixteen, according to Della…and all the smooth bastard is prepared to offer you is a dirty weekend reunion in some godforsaken hole in the hills!' Matt sneered. 'Still, if that's what it takes to turn you on, who am I to interfere?'

'You deliberately let Santino think that you and I were lovers…why did you *do* that?'

Matt grimaced and compressed his mouth, the anger

draining out of him to be replaced by sullen resentment. 'You really don't have the foggiest clue how the average male reacts to being made to look and feel like a fool, do you? Hell, I've had enough of this nonsense! You'd better contact the police and sort it all out...and what about those villas?'

Still in shock, and feeling guilty about the trouble he had been put to on her behalf, she muttered, 'I'm still working on that.'

'This set-up is *work*?' Matt opened the lounge door again and shot her a bitter look. 'I'm glad you're OK, but I feel like wringing your mother's neck for all this!'

Santino was no longer in the hall, and in another thirty seconds Matt, too, was gone, striding out stiff-backed to the hire car parked outside.

Frankie breathed in deeply and then, her mind a whirling turmoil of chaotic thoughts, raced back into the lounge and lifted the phone to contact her mother.

A strange woman answered the phone and questioned her identity. Frankie's voice trembled as she realised she was speaking to a police officer. Only then did the genuine gravity of the situation finally sink in.

Della came on the line, breathless and tearful. 'Are you all right...? Are you *really* all right, Frankie?'

'I'm with Santino, Mum,' Frankie framed shakily, because she was beginning to feel pretty emotional herself. 'You shouldn't have got the police involved...for heaven's sake...'

'If you're with Santino, then you'll know everything,' Della gathered in a strained undertone, and then she went off the line to plead audibly for some privacy. 'Frankie?' she began afresh.

'I was shocked enough to find out that Santino and I were still legally married, but I was devastated when I found out about his financial stake in our lives,' Frankie admitted tautly. 'Della, how *could* you?'

'I couldn't just stand back and allow you to have your

marriage annulled. It would've been like encouraging you to throw solid gold back down the mineshaft! I did it all for *your* sake—'

'Della, please,' Frankie breathed painfully. 'Just be honest.'

'How much more honest can I get? Santino broke your heart and then landed me with a seriously depressed teenager! He deserved to foot the bill for hurting you that much—'

'Mum, I—'

But Della was unstoppable. 'Didn't I do my best for you, Frankie? Didn't I use his money to buy you beautiful clothes and ensure that you lived in luxury? Didn't I throw lots of parties so that you could meet the right sort of people? Is it my fault that none of those things mattered to you and you still moved out as soon as you could?'

'No, but—' Frankie tried to interrupt again, but her mother was now in full angry and defensive flow.

'As for all that rubbish you talked about Santino never having slept with you…do you think I *ever* believed that?' Della vented a sharp laugh of cynical disbelief. 'That was just your pride talking—you trying to cover up the fact that he'd just used you and dumped you again. And Santino thought he could get away with doing precisely that, didn't he? Shove some hush money at me and hang onto his reputation—because he certainly didn't want it coming out that a Vitale had a cute little jailbait bride he'd got bored with!'

Della's stark bitterness on her behalf stunned Frankie. 'But it wasn't like that…'

'You were suicidal, Frankie. He *deserved* to be punished—and I just hope Santino and his filthy rich, snobbish family are cringing at the publicity they're getting now!'

'What p-publicity?' Frankie stammered, with a sick, sinking sensation in her stomach, only vaguely register-

ing the faint click on the line that suggested that someone else had picked up an extension somewhere.

'Look, when you disappeared, I was frantic with
worry!' her mother told her. 'Your father told me loads
of horror stories about Sard vendettas. For all I knew,
Santino had found out where his money was *really* going
and had decided to get rid of you, saving himself the
need to get a very public and expensive divorce from a
wife nobody even knew he had.'

'Mum…this is all so totally insane…' Frankie's head
was banging fit to burst.

'You're very naive, Frankie. The Vitales are a very
powerful and ruthless family, and you can only be an
embarrassment to them. That's why I spiked Santino's
guns for you. Bringing the whole sorry story out into
the open meant you were safe. Right at this minute this
house is being besieged by journalists, and quite a few
of them are Italian… What sort of angle do you want
me to take when I speak to them again?'

Perspiration beading her short upper lip, Frankie
groaned out loud.

Unconcerned, indeed her voice now betraying her excitement, for Della loved to be the centre of attention,
her mother continued inquisitively, 'I mean…how *with*
Santino, are you, darling? Do you want me to say his
family forced the two of you to separate five years
ago…or do you want me to badmouth him as a shameless seducer of teenage girls? It might make a difference
to your divorce settlement—'

Shaking her head in mute disbelief, Frankie muttered
weakly, 'Let me worry about my divorce settlement—'

'Della…' Another voice sliced in with icy precision
on the line, making Frankie's eyes shoot wide in sheer
shock. 'This is Santino. If you speak to one more jour-
nalist, or indeed anyone else who might talk to the paparazzi, I will have you thrown out of that house by the

end of the day. And then I might just take you to court for fraud.'

Appalled silence seethed on the line as both women realised that Santino had been listening in on their dialogue.

'But you're my son-in-law!' Della squawked in aghast protest.

'In this case blood is definitely not thicker than water. *Be warned,*' Santino breathed with chilling exactitude, and the line went dead as Frankie's mother put the phone down without saying another word.

Frankie wheeled round in dizzy confusion as Santino strode into the lounge. Removing the receiver from her damp and loosened grasp, he rammed it back down on the cradle and then, as if that wasn't enough to satisfy him, he yanked the phone cord out of the wall as well. He swung round to face her then.

Uncharacteristically, Frankie shrank. Santino was white with rage beneath his golden skin, his spectacular bone structure hard as iron, shimmering golden eyes slamming into her with ferocious anger.

'That was a most educational call.' Santino's derisive distaste was unconcealed. 'You and your mother have to be the best double act since Bonnie and Clyde. She went to the press for you and now you are happily contemplating your divorce settlement. You conniving little vixen... I should've known you would concentrate on the prospect of eventual profit!'

Pale as milk, Frankie backed off a step. 'Santino...this is all a really ghastly misunderstanding. Mum *has* wildly overreacted, but I think that she honestly believed that she needed to try and protect me—'

'From whom? From *me*? Why should Della need to protect you from me in any way?' Santino demanded with seething bite.

'I never realised that Mum didn't believe me five years ago...about us,' Frankie muttered abstractedly.

'She doesn't even date because she distrusts all men, so I suppose I should have guessed that what happened to me would only make her more bitter. She always used to say that my father and Giles between them wrecked her life, and she thinks you did the same thing to me... Of course, in a way, you *did*—'

'Ensuring that you could live like a princess and attaching no strings to my generosity was...*wrecking* your life?' Santino thrust splayed brown fingers through his luxuriant black hair, his lean dark visage set in lines of outrage. Frankie flinched nervously as he growled something raw under his breath. He fixed burning golden eyes to her transfixed face. '*Sì*, perhaps in this instance the truth does lie where I least want to find it. I did wreck your life in the sense that you are now a twisted version of the woman you might have become.'

'I'm not twisted—'

Santino loosed a harsh laugh of disagreement. 'I gave you into the care of a greedy, selfish woman with her own agenda. If I'd kept you at least you would've hung onto a few morals!'

'I'm not suffering from any shortage in that department, I assure you!' Frankie thrust her chin up, angry colour starting to fire over her cheekbones.

Santino treated her to a slow, insolent sexual appraisal that froze her to the spot. Contemptuous eyes roamed over the deep valley of her breasts, now visible between the parting edges of the robe, to rest on the tantalising twin ripe curves that had been partially revealed. 'Even your lover doesn't ascribe to that belief...'

Frantically twitching the garment back into place and tightening the sash, Frankie said angrily, 'Matt is not and has never been my lover.'

Santino's expressive mouth twisted. 'He is certainly no gentleman if he shares your bed and then chooses to tell me how promiscuous you are.'

Struggling to swallow that insult, Frankie snatched in

a deep shuddering breath and then, without warning, it was as though a bright light exploded inside her head. She was sick and tired of being blamed for everyone else's mistakes, and his attack on her morals was the absolute last straw.

'So what if there have been loads and loads of men in my life?' Frankie flared with angry defiance, well aware that Matt had only made that crack because she had never dated any man for long and her short attention span had offended him, a man who saw that kind of behaviour as a peculiarly male requisite. 'That's none of your business, is it?'

A dark flush slowly rose to accentuate the rigid slant of Santino's slashing cheekbones. For the longest moment he stared at her, eyes as dangerous and cold as black ice. He said nothing.

Frankie broke the screaming silence with a jerky laugh of discomfiture. 'Right, so I'm a tart…big deal!'

But she was no longer able to meet Santino's unsettling gaze. Too late she saw that she had thrown down a gauntlet that he had refused to pick up. Childishly she had tried to shock and she had failed. 'Well, now that we've got that thorny question out of the way,' she continued stiffly, 'don't you think that we ought to be informing the police that I'm here and that there's been the most insane storm in a teacup over nothing?'

'I've already done that. The local police are on their way to confirm your presence…and very soon after that the paparazzi will arrive in their wake,' Santino breathed with grim assurance, already striding out of the room. 'We need to clear out of here fast!'

Unfreezing, Frankie trailed after him and hovered in the doorway of his office, listening to him rap out instructions at speed to someone on the other end of his mobile phone. 'This whole ridiculous mess is your fault,' she accused helplessly as he set the phone aside again. 'If you hadn't lured me out here and set me up with those villas, none of this would ever have happened. And when I go home, how am I supposed to explain all this and you to anybody? You saw how Matt reacted...he thinks this is a truly weird set-up—'

'Weird without sex, boringly conventional *with* it,' Santino slotted in with glancing savagery. 'I do believe it's time I did what I came here to do.'

He strode across to her and, without giving her the slightest hint of his intentions, bent and swept her lithely off her feet and up into his powerful arms.

'Santino...what on earth—?' Frankie gasped.

'I brought you here to put you in the marital bed and enjoy that exquisite body,' Santino reminded her as he started up the stairs with raw determination. 'And I'm still going to achieve that feat *before* we leave.'

'But the police are coming!' Frankie reminded him incredulously, too taken aback by his behaviour even to struggle.

'I think it'll take them quite a while to get here...and if it doesn't they'll have to wait.'

'Wait...while *we*...?' Frankie parroted.

'Why not?' Santino countered, kicking the bedroom door shut behind him and dropping her unceremoniously down on the bed in which she had slept alone yet again the previous night.

Frankie sat up, feverishly pushing flying strands of hair out of her eyes. 'Why *not*?' she repeated in a voice that shook with disbelief. 'Are you out of your mind?'

'No...if I told the typical Sard male that I have waited five years to take physical possession of my beautiful bride, they would probably drive back down the mountain and stay there for at least a month,' Santino breathed with sardonic bite. 'Aside from that, assuming you ultimately intend to be as vocal with the paparazzi as your mother, I wouldn't dream of depriving you of your juiciest source of revelation. No doubt you will be eager to

flog every minute detail of the coming encounter to some
sleazy tabloid when you get home again!'

'You've got absolutely the wrong idea about me...I
wouldn't dream of talking about you to the press!'

'Just the way you swore at the *castello* that you
wouldn't dream of taking my money?' Santino enquired
with splintering and savage condemnation as he ripped
off his shirt and dropped it on the floor. 'You continued
to lie like a pro about your innocence all through the
day. You came up with quite impressive explanations
for almost every charge. You pleaded such complete ignorance and then, when I was on the very *brink* of
awarding you a second hearing, you announced that you
were in on the fraud from the very first day!'

The sight of Santino's bare brown hair-roughened
chest drew Frankie's startled eyes like a magnet to iron
filings. Turning pink, she looked away again and wet her
taut lips with a snaking flick of her tongue. She was
appalled by that masterly summing-up of her credibility
in his eyes. Santino didn't trust a word she said, which
wasn't surprising when she recalled the number of times
she had changed her tune that day, before she'd finally
shouldered Della's guilt in an effort to protect the older
woman from the full onslaught of Santino's cold and
deadly fury.

It felt like the worst possible moment to be suddenly
wishing that she could now tell him the truth. Santino
had to despise Della even more since he had heard her
talking on the phone in that coy, calculating way. And,
where once Frankie had lied to save her parent out of
knee-jerk loyalty, now, ironically, she had a stronger
motivation. Della might not be the ideal parent she had
once longed to have, but today Frankie had learnt something that touched that sore place in her heart.

Evidently her mother had strongly sympathised with
her daughter's misery five years ago, and would probably have done so more vocally had Frankie been pre-

pared to confide more fully in her. Had that happened, their relationship might never have become so detached. In that one field alone, perhaps they had something in common.

'I am really not the person you think I am,' Frankie said shakily, tilting back her head again to look at Santino as she sat on the bed. 'I wish I could tell you something more than that, but just at this moment—'

'Just at this moment you would tell me anything it suited you to tell me.'

Breathless, and abruptly shorn of the ability to vocalise, Frankie focused on Santino as he stripped off a pair of silk boxer shorts and stood there magnificently nude and dauntingly uninhibited. The involuntary victim of a scorching attack of shyness, she removed her attention from the most eye-catching male attribute on display, struggling to swallow on shock and failing dismally. She had always wondered, and now she was receiving the opportunity to forever satisfy all female curiosity, and yet she found that she just couldn't look again because she was gripped by such intense self-consciousness.

'Santino…' she croaked.

'Forget it… I won't believe you have a shy or modest bone in your entire body,' Santino delivered fiercely, coming down on the bed and curving strong hands round her forearms to pull her towards him. 'Not a woman who boasts about the number of men she's had and offers me anything I want in bed without even pausing to consider the risk that I might want something she wouldn't be prepared to give—'

'Might you?' Frankie slotted in helplessly, bare inches away from shimmering golden eyes that seemed to burn over every inch of her exposed skin.

'What do you think?' Santino traded with silken scorn. 'I think possibly you could teach me a thing or two.'

'I'm not in the mood right now—'

'I'll put you in the mood, *cara*. I also think I should have tipped you head-first into the horse trough to sober up last night! You suck up sympathy like a vacuum cleaner, you always did, and you don't deserve my care and consideration.'

Releasing her arms, Santino tugged free the sash at her slender waist in one smooth movement.

The robe fell open. Frankie froze, breath feathering in her convulsive throat, heart racing so fast she felt light-headed.

Santino ran burnished and unashamedly hungry eyes over the enticing feminine curves he had revealed. He reached an assured hand up into her tumbling bright mane of hair and slowly, sensually drew her down onto the pillows. She arrived there with a stifled gasp, just in time to see him close one beautifully shaped hand over the pale swell of one full breast. She trembled, wide-eyed, shaken by both sight and sensation. The heat of his rawly masculine body against her cooler, slighter frame, even the fairness of her skin against his lean, sun-darkened length, was as instinctively enthralling as the expert fingers which rose to caress the pouting pink nipple.

A low, jerky sigh escaped her, her head falling back as the sweet ache of her sensitive flesh made her clench her teeth, blanking out her mind to everything but the power of sensation he possessed, and when he bent his dark head and delicately employed his teeth and his tongue on the same straining rosy bud she moaned out loud.

'What a temptress you are, Francesca,' Santino breathed in a tone of roughened discovery. 'You surrender yourself so completely to pleasure.'

The fog in her brain was pierced by sudden shame. Her lashes lifted again just as Santino pushed a supporting arm beneath her and eased her free of her robe, to cast it carelessly aside. He thrust the bedding back, tumbling her onto a crisp white cotton sheet scented with the faint evocative aroma of crushed rosemary.

Santino focused on her intently, his strong dark features taut. 'Rosemary for fertility—not a concern that I assume I need to consider with you…?'

Frankie's gaze was blank, inward-looking. A tide of burning colour washed over her skin because she wasn't listening; she was picturing herself just seconds earlier, a willing, wanton captive to what he could make her feel. And yet wasn't this what she wanted too? This driving hunger of the flesh satisfied so that she could be free again, free as she had never been in five long years? Inwardly she repeated the comforting mantra that had strengthened her only the day before. Making love with Santino would close this chapter in her life and then she would move on.

'And you still blush…a charming if deceptive consequence of that superb English-rose skin,' Santino contended, brushing away the top sheet she had automatically drawn over herself so that he could feast his attention upon her again.

Frankie stared up at him, as entrapped as if he had her in chains, shyness overpowered by her incredibly deep and strong craving for his admiration. It made her feel so good about herself, so happy. Breasts that had seemed too full for her slender stature, hips that had seemed too angular no longer mattered. Her own new and wondrous sense of perfection was born in that instant in Santino's deeply appreciative appraisal.

'You're exquisite, *cara mia*,' Santino murmured intently. 'At this moment, I don't care about anything else.'

'There *is* nothing else,' Frankie whispered, thinking that there would be just this one time and then they would part, for he had already referred to their leaving the village. A hazy image vaguely reminiscent of *Brief Encounter* seduced her with its drama and romance.

Her hand lifted and curved over a broad brown shoulder, fluttering in an instinctive wondering caress over smooth, taut skin covering a spectacular blending of bone and muscle. It felt so daring and yet so right, here in this bed and in this house, the world shut outside, just the way it might have been five years ago—just the way it *should* have been, she reflected helplessly. A spontaneous and natural event because she had never been infatuated, she had been deeply in love. And, just as then, looking at Santino melted her deep down inside. Her breathing fractured, her quivering body clenching on the all-pervasive sense of dissolving liquidity between her thighs.

'When you look at me like that,' Santino confided, his deep, dark drawl like abrasive sand on silk, 'I want to forget every preliminary I ever learned and fall on you like a sex-starved teenager.'

'Do you?' A dreamy smile of satisfaction curved Frankie's generous mouth, the last shred of uncertainty forgotten as she rejoiced in the sheer power of being a woman.

Santino leant over her and kissed her with a plundering urgency that both shook and excited her simultaneously. He wound a ruthless hand into her hair and held her captive, crushing her lips and invading her mouth with an erotic thoroughness that swiftly changed the status quo—because she became a creature of all feeling and no thought, dragged down into shivering excitement by his innate sensuality.

His hands were slightly rough against her softer skin, the knowing exploration of his fingers over her achingly tender breasts a tormenting pleasure as she strained helplessly up to him, her whole body awash with response and reaction to his every tiny move and caress. She felt dominated and confined and she liked it, and she laced her seeking fingers ecstatically into his thick black hair, holding him tightly to her.

He dragged himself free, shone an innately ruthless smile of satisfaction over her confused face. Her treacherous heart contracted in response.

He looked so dangerous, his slashing confidence unhidden. 'I'm not going anywhere, *cara*...your hunger is the one true gift you have to give me and the only thing you cannot lie about or control. The completeness of your surrender will be my triumph.'

Her stomach twisted, apprehension threatening to break through the unstoppable waves of hunger that controlled her as surely as he did. But with a soft taunting laugh Santino kissed her again, with all the fiery carnal expertise she was defenceless against. Her body burned, no longer willing or able to do her bidding. She was possessed by her own need, her own ever more desperate hunger. She wanted to sink inside his skin and share it with him.

His mouth teased at the straining buds of her swollen breasts. Slow, sure fingers skimmed through the damp curls that guarded her femininity to touch where only he had ever touched. The sensitivity of her flesh was almost unbearable and the explosive, agonising pleasure which seized Frankie in its relentless hold made her jerk and twist and whimper in mindless abandonment.

'You're so ready for me,' Santino groaned.

His lean, strong features harsh and intent in passion, he rose over her, lifting her trembling thighs back and settling himself fluidly between them. As she felt him, hot and urgent and alarmingly male against her tender entrance, Frankie gasped and tensed, and yet with every contrary fibre of her being she would have died of frustration had he stopped. Then he moved, and pleasure splintered into shocking pain as he thrust deep and a startled cry was wrenched from her.

For an instant Santino fell still. He surveyed her with

lancing golden eyes that scorched like flames over her
hectically flushed and shaken face. 'If ever anyone got
the punishment they deserved for lying...' he breathed,
unexpectedly deepening his invasion with a powerful
twist of his hips. 'I would have been slow and gentle if
I had known the truth.'

So intent was Frankie on the alien intrusion wreaking
such upheaval inside her tormentingly sensitised body,
she barely caught his words. She was afraid to move
until the pain faded, and then she gazed up at him in
open surprise. 'It feels so strange,' she whispered.

'It gets to feel good,' Santino promised, with a reluctant laugh and a slanting, almost tender smile.

She couldn't imagine that, but then it was happening
and suddenly she couldn't concentrate any more and that
instant of control was wrested from her again. Her whole
being centred on his every movement, over her, inside
her, and the raw power of his possession filled her with
wild energy and impatience. It was timeless, utterly absorbing, and she lived each second on an edge of excruciating all-encompassing craving and then she was splintering and shuddering, flung in shock to the furthest
boundaries of pleasure. With a hungry growl of release,
Santino followed her there, and when she surfaced from
that drugging languor of satiation she found herself
clutching him with a sense of feverish possessiveness.

As he freed her partially of his weight, Frankie yanked
her clinging hands from him. That was inappropriate
now that the lovemaking was over, she told herself.

Outrageously unfazed by any concept of what was or
was not appropriate in the circumstances, Santino rolled
her over and contemplated the sheet with impossible
cool, not a muscle moving on his vibrantly handsome
face. 'Welcome back, Santa Claus and the Tooth Fairy,'
he mused softly. 'Miracles do happen against all the
odds.'

Silence stretched and strained like an elastic band

drawn to breaking point. With a galling air of expectancy, Santino took in her outraged look and waited.

'I despise you for this most of all!' Frankie shot at him, feeling naked inside and out, exposed as a fraud where she had most wished to pose as an equal.

As she attempted to shoot off the edge of the bed, a strong hand restrained her. 'My bride, the fake seductress. No wonder you got drunk last night. You needed Dutch courage because you weren't quite sure what to do with me,' Santino breathed with grim amusement, stunning dark eyes raking over her hot and furious face.

Without even thinking about it, Frankie swung up a punitive hand and tried to slap him. Instead she found herself pressed back to the mattress, shocked by the speed of his reactions even as he glowered down at her. 'No,' Santino said succinctly. 'Lash out with your tongue, not your hands, and comfort yourself with the knowledge that I only hurt you because you lied to me.'

Shock surged back over the edge into sheer ungovernable rage. Frankie struggled to free herself from his strong hands and failed. 'Let go of me!' she railed at him, her strained voice breaking.

'My wildcat wife.' Santino surveyed her with a disturbing light of understanding in his shrewd assessment. 'When I crack the surface you are as hopelessly volatile as ever you were. Passion will always betray you—'

'Damn you, Santino…shut up!' she hissed.

'As long as I live, I will never forget you shouting across the lobby that day in Cagliari. ''You were mine,'' you screamed. ''Now I wish you were dead!'' And you meant every word of it,' Santino mused reflectively. 'If you had had a gun you would have shot me—because if you couldn't have me nobody else could be allowed to have me. In the space of a heartbeat, love turned to violent hatred…'

Shutting him out with her lashes, all temper quelled by the unbearably painful reminder of her devastation that day, Frankie said unsteadily, 'I want to get up and pack now.'

'Good idea,' Santino conceded, releasing her in a cool, almost careless movement, as if he could not quite understand why he should still have been holding her close. 'The helicopter should be here soon.'

'Helicopter?' she queried, and then she remembered the phone call he had made downstairs and muttered, 'Yes, of course.' A helicopter to whisk them away at speed to the airport, where they would each go their separate ways—for anything else was now impossible. The publicity, the huge furore Della had ignited would follow them both, and Santino naturally wouldn't want to encourage greater media interest by keeping her with him.

She ran a bath for herself and climbed in, wincing at the unaccustomed soreness she could feel. Herself and Santino? It was over, totally, absolutely and for ever over. She would never see him again. Frankie stared for a long, timeless moment into space, and then her eyes prickled hotly and stung and the tears surged up and gushed like a waterfall. Perfectly natural, grieving for the end of an era, she told herself feverishly, snatching up a towel and burying her face in it as a choking sob swelled up inside her constricted chest.

'Mourning your lost virginity?'

Startled by the interruption, Frankie dropped the towel in the bathwater. 'What are you doing in here?' she demanded strickenly.

'I need a shower…only one bathroom.' Making that reminder, Santino gazed down at her, hard dark eyes sharp enough to strip paint. 'If you want to say goodbye to your family in person, you had better hurry. Otherwise you can call them from Rome.'

'R-Rome?' Frankie repeated in a daze, pausing in the very act of plastering the soaking wet towel to her bare breasts. 'But I'm not going to Rome…'

'Oh, yes, you are,' Santino confirmed steadily. 'Where else did you think you might be going?'

'I thought…I thought we were heading for the airport and then splitting up… I thought I was going home—'

'You thought wrong. I haven't had my three weeks yet…and, by the way, the clock only started ticking when we climbed into bed an hour ago,' Santino imparted as he reached into the shower cubicle and switched on the water. 'You get your timesheet docked for nerves and insobriety.'

'You can't want to keep me with you after all the publicity there's been!' Frankie was reeling with renewed shock, a state that Santino appeared equal to keeping her in almost continually. The pressure of never really knowing what was likely to happen next was starting to wear down her nerves.

Santino shrugged out of his robe and let it fall to the floor, gloriously unconcerned by his nudity. '*Cara*…I don't care if I have to pitch a tent at the top of Everest. You're putting in your time…' He glanced back at her, classic profile hard and implacable. 'I can only hope that I don't live to discover that you're likely to be around even longer…'

'I beg your pardon?' Frankie whispered without comprehension.

'Unless I'm very much mistaken we just had sex without precautions.' Santino sent her a charged look, obsidian in its chilling gravity. 'When I asked you if I needed to worry about your fertility, I took your silence for confirmation that I *didn't* need to protect us both from that risk.'

'I don't remember you asking me anything of the sort!' Frankie gasped. 'You mean you didn't…? No, you didn't…' As she answered that question for herself her voice died away, and she shivered in the cold, clammy clasp of the sopping towel, gripped by panic at the threat of an accidental pregnancy by a male who despised her.

That she was actually married to that same male didn't seem remotely relevant.

'And if your misleading silence was less a mistake than a deliberate attempt to prolong a most profitable association with me…you've made a cardinal error which you will undoubtedly live to regret,' Santino assured her, jawline hard as iron.

An almost hysterical giggle feathered dangerously in Frankie's dry throat. She surveyed him with huge, unwittingly fascinated eyes. Right then she was wondering if the blood of the suspicious Borgias ran in Santino's veins. Here she was, still in shock at the realisation that there had been a misunderstanding and that they had made love without contraception, but Santino's serpentine reasoning processes were infinitely darker and more cynical than her own. He already suspected her of having deliberately deceived him into running that risk.

'I won't even dignify that accusation with an answer,' she returned tightly.

'Even if you prove to be pregnant, I will *still* divorce you,' Santino gritted with ferocious bite as he strode into the shower. 'Three weeks and you're out, bag and baggage…no matter what!'

'Santino…' Frankie breathed, and then she stopped because she heard the betrayingly emotional wobble affecting her diction. Reluctant to probe the complex and painfully confusing storm of emotions attacking her, she chose only to voice her impatience with his fatalistic conviction that one little oversight would unerringly lead to conception.

'I'm quite sure that any egg of mine would have more taste than even to consider an approach from anything with the Vitale signature on it…' Frankie countered curtly. 'In fact, I'm utterly convinced that right now your reproductive cells are fighting a pitched and losing battle in hostile territory and wishing very much that they had stayed home!'

'I can only hope…for both our sakes…that you're right,' Santino delivered rawly, ramming shut the doors on the corner cubicle with a suppressed violence that fully illustrated his mood.

As she clambered out of the bath, dashing tears from her eyes, Frankie scolded herself furiously for her own over-sensitivity. It was stupid to feel so totally gutted by Santino's appalled reaction to the risk that she might conceive. After all, how likely was it that they might be unlucky? And why *should* his attitude hurt and wound her? Why should it feel like the ultimate rejection? Goodness knew, she would be climbing the walls too if that misunderstanding of theirs led to such a consequence!

CHAPTER EIGHT

'BUT your passport is in the name of Caparelli, *signora*,' the portly little local police inspector remarked with a frown of surprise. 'Indeed it still carries the designation of a single woman.'

'Francesca applied for a British passport in her maiden name shortly before our marriage.' As Santino spoke, Frankie studied him covertly. He was sheathed in a stupendously well-cut pearl-grey suit that framed his broad shoulders, lean hips and long, long legs to quite spectacular effect, and she was finding it a really horrendous challenge to look anywhere else.

'Perhaps the continued use of Caparelli was intended as a security precaution?' the older man hazarded uncertainly, evidently aware of the kidnapping that had once occurred in the Vitale family. He returned the item to Frankie with a wry shrug of acceptance. 'It should be brought up to date now. Your face has been splashed all over the newspapers and the television screen. It is sadly ironic, *signor*…your illustrious family are famed for their zealous protection of their privacy but your wife couldn't walk down a street anywhere in Italy today without being instantly recognised as a Vitale.'

Santino tensed, his strong face darkening at the assurance. Frankie was certain he had to be appalled by that information. Discretion, yes, he had mentioned the necessity of discretion at their very first meeting in La Rocca, only then she had not grasped his true meaning because she hadn't had a clue that Santino belonged to one of the wealthiest and most newsworthy families in

Europe. Nor could she even believe as yet that she was really to fly to Rome with him.

'It's crazy to force me to accompany you back to Rome,' Frankie contended half under her breath as she watched the policeman climb back into his car, his subordinate, who had played no part in the interview, taking the wheel.

'When you steal a ride on someone else's rollercoaster, Francesca, you can't expect it to stop just because you find it scary that events are moving out of your control.'

Frankie lost colour at that perceptive stab, her stomach twisting. The tension between them nagged like toothache at her raw nerve-endings. The racket of a helicopter coming in low over the valley broke the silence and she turned towards the lounge window, eager to make use of any distraction. But long brown fingers closed with ruthless precision over one slim, taut shoulder and prevented her retreat.

Her head whipped round, tilting back to look up at Santino. 'I *am* in control!' she informed him doggedly, digging her unsteady hands deep into the pockets of her loose ankle-length summer dress. 'And I am not scared—'

'But you *should* be,' Santino emphasised, his rich, dark drawl feathering down her rigid spine like a dangerous storm warning that ironically both threatened and thrilled. Stunning dark eyes raked over her defensive face. 'For there is one weakness we do not share...unlike you, I will never be passion's slave. When it is time for us to part, what will you do if you find yourself possessed by a devastatingly strong need for our affair to continue?'

Imprisoned within inches of his lean, muscular body and painfully, newly aware of his erotic masculine power in a way that lacerated her pride and filled her with foreboding, Frankie stared up at him, appalled to feel a deep inner trembling begin and spread a terrifying woolly weakness through her lower limbs. 'I think I'd cut my throat!' she countered with fiery disdain.

Santino's mesmeric eyes glittered, his shapely, sensual mouth slashing into a reluctant smile of appreciation. 'Kill or cure, all or nothing...how little you have changed, *cara*. But unfortunately life rarely makes one's choices so simple.'

'It's always simple if you want it to be,' Frankie told him between gritted teeth as she fought the onslaught of that shattering sexual awareness. Her pulses were racing so fast she felt dizzy and her hands were balled into fists inside her pockets for fear that she might reach for him. Like a mindless addict she wanted to move closer and drink in the hot, achingly seductive scent of him, seek contact, actual *physical* contact to satisfy the treacherous craving that made her breath catch in her throat and her sensitive breasts tingle and swell.

A long forefinger stroked down the side of her face and her green eyes darkened and centred with compulsive intensity on the lean dark features above hers. 'Sexual hunger is never simple because we are not animals, mating without thought or feeling at nature's behest...how innocent you are in spite of your avarice. You can't even admit your own ignorance. But the higher you climb on that ladder of self-deception, the harder you will fall.'

His thumb grazed the corner of her full, tremulous lips and then almost lazily slid to probe within. Involuntarily her languorous eyes slid shut, her lips converging hungrily on that intrusive digit, the lancing bitter-sweet pain of that hunger shrilling through her slender frame, making every muscle fiercely taut with anticipation.

'And with the smallest encouragement...such a natural-born temptress,' Santino completed, his accent thickening as he closed one impatient hand over her hip to yank her closer.

The knocker on the front door sounded with thunderous urgency. Frankie almost leapt out of her skin. As her shaken eyes slowly opened, Santino was already striding out to the hall to answer the door. A powerfully built man in a dark suit, whom Santino addressed as Nardo, swept up the cases at the foot of the stairs. Of course, Frankie registered, like someone surfacing from a heavily drugged slumber, the helicopter had landed and it was time for them to leave.

She pressed moist palms to her hot cheeks. She had not meant to give Santino such power over her, had never dreamt that her surrender might weaken her defences even more. And he was wrong when he still called her innocent because she was no longer the optimistic fool who had fondly imagined that going to bed with Santino would magically exorcise her emotional turmoil.

'You'll visit again soon?' Maddalena pressed anxiously, as her great-aunts and grandfather stood waiting to see them off.

'Francesca's place is with her husband and Santino is a very busy man,' Teresa scolded her sister. 'Who else do you know who has to call for a helicopter because he can't spare the time to drive down the mountain?'

Her grandfather took her aside and treated her to a troubled and questioning look. 'Santino usually says his goodbyes personally.'

And the cruel weight of reality almost crushed Frankie then. Santino would not be returning to the village again. And the next time she visited she would come alone, bearing news which would hit her far from liberal-minded family hard. A broken marriage and a divorce in the offing. That would shame and distress her great-aunts and outrage and disappoint her grandfather, who had grown infinitely more fond and proud of Santino than he had ever been of his own unreliable and selfish son. And they would all blame her because she simply could not imagine them blaming Santino for anything...

Frankie fell asleep during the flight. When Santino woke her up, she glanced out through the window beside her and was thoroughly disorientated by the view, for they were certainly not at Rome's Fiumicino airport; the helicopter appeared to be surrounded by a boundless expanse of lush green grass.

'You look as messy as a child returning from a day on the beach,' Santino censured as he lifted her down onto solid ground again. He looked unusually tense. As he scanned the drowsy blankness of her face, his beautiful mouth tightened even more. He paused to brush straying strands of bright hair off her brow and make a somewhat pointless attempt to smooth down her badly creased cotton dress.

Smothering a yawn, Frankie let herself be walked at a smart pace across the lawn. Yes, it was a lawn, definitely a lawn—well, possibly more of a stretch of parkland really, she finally decided an instant before she fell to an abrupt halt to gape at the quite spectacular building basking in the late-afternoon heat about a hundred yards ahead of them.

'My home,' Santino advanced, a firm hand on her elbow urging her on.

'Your home? Where on earth are we?' she mumbled in a daze.

'About thirty miles from Rome. The paparazzi will not disturb us here. The estate boundaries are constantly patrolled and the surveillance technology which supports the security presence is of the highest calibre. A leaf doesn't drop from a tree at the Villa Fontana without someone knowing about it.'

Fascinated, Frankie absorbed the breathtaking beauty of the centuries-old country mansion before her. A two-storey central block with an elaborate but very pretty façade was flanked on either side by curved wings creating an inviting sunlit piazza to the front. At the great domed and arched entrance beyond, the longest limousine Frankie had ever seen sat with blacked-out windows.

'You're about to meet my parents,' Santino imparted without a flicker of expression, but his strong profile was taut. 'You should feel honoured. Evidently they have dragged themselves all the way from Switzerland to make their shock, horror and disapproval known.'

Catapulted with a vengeance back into full awareness, Frankie gulped. 'Your...*parents*?'

'Once you dreamt of meeting them,' Santino reminded her lethally. 'You imagined how you would exchange recipes and knitting patterns with my mother. You wondered if you should write to them to reassure them that I was being wonderfully well looked after. And how heartbroken you assumed my poor mother must be because she lived too far away to even attend her own son's wedding—'

'Don't remind me!' Frankie exclaimed, her lovely face burning with chagrin as they mounted the steps to pass under the entrance arch.

Through the open doors beyond they entered a magnificent long hallway adorned with marble pillars and statues in alcoves. Thoroughly intimidated by the grandeur, Frankie dropped her volume to that of a frantic whisper. 'All right, so I had about as much idea of your background then as a little green man landing from Mars, but I can't meet your parents now, looking like this!' She glanced down at herself to wonder in fierce frustration why she hadn't long since binned a dress that resembled a crumpled dishcloth after a few hours of wear.

'Francesca...it really wouldn't matter if you were a saint of stunning perfection and poise. They would find your very existence no more palatable,' Santino admitted with a wry twist of his mouth.

'Why didn't you warn me that your parents might be here waiting?'

'They rarely visit me. But scurrilous publicity involving the family name would appear to have a very enlivening effect upon them.'

'Look, you should deal with your parents on your own,' Frankie muttered. 'Not much point in getting them all worked up when I'm not staying around, is there?'

'That's my business, *not* theirs,' Santino decreed with harsh emphasis, and he curved an imprisoning arm against her spine.

An anxious-looking little woman in a smart black dress was stationed outside the last door to the left at the end of the hall. She burst into frantic, low-pitched Italian. Santino made smooth, soothing responses.

'My housekeeper, Lina. I'll introduce you later. Visitors who refuse all refreshment unnerve her, and my mother can be rather intimidating,' Santino confided in exasperation as he spread open the door on a very grand drawing room.

Her mouth dry as a bone, Frankie focused on the small, dark, exquisitely dressed older woman seated in a stiff-backed chair. 'Intimidating' was the word. The ice-blue of her suit matched her eyes, and Frankie finally saw the source of Santino's superb bone structure. A tall distinguished man with white hair turned from the windows. He held himself with the same unbending reserve and formality as his wife.

'Francesca…' Santino murmured flatly. 'Allow me to introduce you to my parents…Sonia and Alvaro.'

'I will accept no introduction,' Sonia Vitale asserted glacially. 'Explain yourself, Santino! How *could* you disgrace us by allowing your outrageous association with this woman to be exposed by the press?'

'We understood that this unfortunate affair had been buried some years ago,' Alvaro Vitale advanced.

'I made no such promise,' Santino countered levelly. 'Francesca is my wife and I expect you to treat her with all due respect and civility.'

Sonia Vitale ran coldly outraged eyes over Frankie. Her lip curling, she turned her imperious head away again in a gesture of lofty dismissal. 'I will never receive that woman into my home as my daughter-in-law.'

'Then you will not receive me either,' Santino responded harshly. 'And I shouldn't think that would be too great a sacrifice. After all, you only see me once a year at Christmas as it is.'

Frankie sent Santino an astonished glance and then focused on his mother again, shocked by the bitter hostility the older woman could not conceal when she looked at her son.

'You must see that this is an inappropriate marriage,' Alvaro Vitale intervened afresh. 'I intend no disrespect towards your wife, but on one count your mother must surely be excused her frank speech. Francesca's background scarcely equips her to take her place in our family—'

'We are not royalty, Papà,' Santino incised grimly.

'It is a waste of time to try to reason with you, Santino. You could never be anything other than a disappointment to me,' his mother condemned cruelly. 'But you betray your brother's memory with this insult of a marriage—'

Beside her, Frankie felt Santino's big, powerful frame tense like a cat about to spring, but a split second earlier she had felt him recoil from his mother's attack. She stiffened, fighting the most extraordinary urge to speak up in his defence.

His mother continued to survey him with cold condemnation. 'I would remind you that you will always walk in Rico's shadow, Santino. All that was once his has come to you. Honour should demand that you make sacrifices in his memory. And Rico would never have married a social inferior. Rico never once brought shame on the Vitale name. He was too proud of our ancestry.'

'I am not and I can never be Rico, Mamma,' Santino countered wearily, the long fingers resting on Frankie's slim hip biting painfully into her flesh.

Sonia Vitale rose from her chair. 'How you do love to state the obvious,' she responded cuttingly. 'You knew it was our dearest wish that you should marry Melina. Instead you have made a mockery of us all. When you can bring Melina to me as your bride, I will see you again...not before.'

Her husband moved forward, his strain now palpable in spite of his efforts to retain his impassivity. 'Santino...may I have a word with you in private?' he enquired. 'You will excuse us, Francesca?'

'I will wait in the car, Alvaro,' Sonia announced, and she swept past them all with her regal head held high.

Without even considering what she was about to do, her sole driving purpose one of furious incomprehension, Frankie pulled free of Santino's loosened grip and sped in his mother's wake, pausing only to jerk shut the drawing-room door behind her.

'Why don't you *love* him?' Frankie demanded fiercely of the older woman in the echoing hallway.

Sonia Vitale came to a startled halt and gazed back at Frankie over her shoulder in complete shock. 'I beg your p-pardon?' she murmured with an incredulous shake in her well-modulated voice as she turned. 'Santino is my son. *Of course* I love my—'

'No, you don't!' Frankie contradicted her, her eyes bright with condemnation. 'You look at him like you hate and resent him...you deliberately try to hurt him... All I want to know is why. *Why?* Santino is pretty damned wonderful in an awful lot of ways. He's clever and caring and honest. Most mothers would be really proud to have a son like that...'

Every scrap of colour draining from her still beautiful features, the older woman backed slowly away from her. A stunned and appalled look of confusion had blossomed in her eyes. 'How dare you attack me...how dare you say such things?'

Suddenly equally shattered by her own behaviour, Frankie froze and flushed a hot self-conscious pink. She could not even understand what had driven her into forcing such a confrontation. Out of nowhere had come this ferocious sense of angry protectiveness and it had sent her hurtling into pursuit like a guided missile, for certainly she hadn't stopped and thought about what she was about to do...no, not even for a sensible second. And what had she done now but pointlessly enrage Santino's mother more and make an already bad situation worse?

'So my son has married a real little fishwife who fights for him...like a vixen protecting her cub. But Santino wouldn't thank you for abusing me.' Sonia drew on her gloves in a series of jerky little movements that betrayed her distress and her eyes never once met Frankie's again. 'In fact he would devour you alive because naturally he *loves* and reveres his mother. And I see, not without some surprise after reading your mother's highly unladylike revelations in print, that you genuinely *do* love my son...but you are only a brief aberration in Santino's life and will fortunately soon be gone.'

Frankie flinched as if the smaller woman had slyly slid a knife between her ribs, but Sonia had already spun away from her again.

'You should have been his mistress, not his wife. Melina would have accepted that. We would *all* have accepted that,' Sonia imparted curtly. 'But it is too late for that resolution now. You have lost the anonymity so necessary to that position. When Santino tires of you, as

he inevitably will, and turns back to Melina, you will
see then that I am right, for you will lose him altogether.'

As the older woman walked away, Frankie reeled
clumsily round behind one of the pillars and pressed her
hot, damp forehead to the cold marble. She felt as if she
had gone ten rounds with a champion boxer and her very
flesh had been pummelled from her bones. No, she did
not love Santino...no, *no*, she did not! She was a whole
lot brighter than the teenager she had once been. Yes,
maybe she was—maybe she was more worldly-wise, an
inner voice conceded, but there was no denying that at
the age of sixteen sheer gut instinct had prompted her to
fix her affections on one hell of a guy.

Because Santino *was* one hell of a guy, although not
in the mood he had been in since she had successfully
convinced him that she was the lowest, greediest and
most ungrateful female in existence. But as he *could* be,
as he had once been, and as he had promised to be that
very first day they met again in La Rocca, before everything had gone wrong, he was still so incredibly special
and important to her.

Dear heaven, I *do* still love Santino, Frankie registered
in horror. I have no hope of getting him out of my system. He's just *in* there...inside my heart...inside my
head, as much a part of me as my own flesh.

In the midst of that unwelcome flood of self-
revelation, Alvaro Vitale emerged from the drawing
room and strode past, mercifully without seeing her lurk-
ing behind the pillar.

Looking very pale and feeling unusually uncertain of
herself, indeed almost crushingly shy, Frankie finally
moved back into the room the older man had vacated.
Santino didn't notice her hesitant entry and hovering
stance about twenty feet from him. He was pouring himself what looked like a pretty stiff drink. Cradling the
whisky tumbler in one lean brown hand, he strode rest-
lessly over to the windows and stood there, wide shoul-

ders rigid with livewire tension, long legs braced slightly apart.

Her dazed eyes roamed over his arrogant dark head and that bold, strong profile silhouetted against the light. How could she love a male capable of ruthlessly using her body to satisfy lust alone? How could she love a man who could separate all emotion from sex and without conscience play on her inexperience, susceptibility and, cruellest of all, her deep fear of being out of control?

Oh, so easily, she answered for herself. For this was the dark side of Santino's powerful personality and forceful temperament, a side he had never shown her before but which she should always have known existed. He could not have borne to let her go unpunished and he could not forgive greed or deception. Strong men had strong principles. And without those principles she would have found Santino infinitely less attractive.

She cleared her throat gruffly and asked the first question which came to mind. 'Who is Melina?'

Santino glanced almost unseeingly at her and then away again, his preoccupation patent. 'A friend...as dear as a daughter to my mother.'

The worst of Frankie's tension evaporated. Not an explanation couched in terms likely to drive her mad with jealousy, she thought with a sensation of powerful relief. 'And Rico...? He was your brother?' she prompted tautly as Santino's dark head whipped instantaneously back to her, his beautiful dark eyes filled with a deep, tormented sadness and defensive bitterness.

'You know, you never, ever mentioned having had a brother,' Frankie remarked, choosing her words very carefully but wholly focused on a need to know what could bring such an expression to Santino's face.

'Rico died the year before I met you. He was ten years older than me,' Santino admitted grudgingly.

'What happened?'

For several thunderously tense seconds Santino fixed his attention on the window again. Then he shrugged with something less than his usual fluidity. 'Rico took me climbing in the Alps. The climb should have been abandoned on the second day. Conditions were poor and the weather was changing. But Rico—' He breathed stiltedly. 'Rico was a daredevil determined not to be beaten by the elements. An avalanche hit us. He saved my life at the cost of his own.'

'Oh, God…' Frankie framed sickly, out of her depth with words. What she most needed was the freedom to rush across the room and wrap comforting arms around him, but she was utterly terrified of the rejection she was convinced she would receive. 'That…that must have devastated your family—'

'Sì…the wrong son came back down the mountain—'

'Don't say things like that,' Frankie begged with a superstitious shiver. 'If your parents somehow left you with the idea that you were more expendable than your older brother, that could only have been an accidental result of their grief and—'

Santino dealt her a winging look of contempt. 'Tell me, were you or were you not present when Sonia was delivering her opinion of my worth in comparison to my late brother's?'

Frankie couldn't meet his gaze. She shifted awkwardly.

'And Rico *was* a wonderful man. My mother worshipped the ground he walked on. Hell, so did I!' Santino gritted. 'He was an unparalleled success at being all things to all people. When he died he left a great yawning hole in our lives and family unity vanished. I found myself being treated like the living dead. My mother could not forgive me for surviving at Rico's expense.'

Since that was more or less Frankie's estimate of Sonia Vitale's feelings as well, she averted guilty eyes from his. Santino would naturally scorn empty protests.

And for the first time she understood what might have drawn him so frequently to his great-uncle's isolated village in Sardinia. Father Vassari had been a kind and practical man. Santino had been treated like a pariah by his parents while he was still only a teenager. He must've been comforted by the old man's continuing affection, and no doubt his reassurance that Rico's death had been in no way his fault.

She was warmed by that image but troubled and hurt by it too, for once *she* had eagerly shared her every anxiety and fear with Santino. Yet he had never told her about his brother, never once risked burdening her with anything she might not have been able to handle. More than everything else that underlined how unequal their relationship had been then. He had put her needs and concerns ahead of his own. Always. He had been the giver, she the taker…and the long-overdue acknowledgement shook Frankie to her very depths.

'All of a sudden you're very quiet,' Santino remarked softly.

Squirming with discomfiture, Frankie lifted her bright head again. Santino was already crossing the room to her. Unsettled by his sudden proximity, threatened by her new awareness of how much she loved him, she collided involuntarily with fiercely intent dark golden eyes.

'But the act of confession must indeed be good for the soul,' Santino informed her with husky conviction as he stretched out confident hands to ease her into intimate connection with his hard, muscular frame. 'Or perhaps it is the wealth of compassion you contrive to suggest with those wonderfully eloquent green eyes. Whatever… *Dio*… I have an overwhelming need to lose myself now in sexual oblivion!'

CHAPTER NINE

'SANTINO…?' Frankie gasped breathlessly, taken aback by the volatile charge of sexual hunger in his brilliant gaze.

'You want me too,' Santino groaned, backing her up against the door without hesitation and dropping his dark head to press his mouth with burning eroticism to the sensitive skin of her throat. He sent a shiver of such electrified heat through her slender length that her legs shook and threatened to crumple beneath her.

'Don't you, *cara*?' he prompted with blatant assurance.

'Yes…' she muttered unsteadily, painfully conscious of her inability to resist him. 'Yes…'

Santino muttered something raw and husky in Italian and closed his hands over the swelling curve of her hips, spreading his muscular thighs to bring her into contact with the rampant thrust of his erection. As he trembled against her, answering fire sprang up low in her belly. Her entire body burned, infused with a surging, desperate need she could not fight.

He skimmed sure hands down her quivering thighs to part them and raised her dress with summary masculine impatience. Expert fingers teased the heated core of her through the thin barrier of her briefs and he vented a husky sigh of satisfaction as he discovered the dampness she could neither control nor conceal. Frankie shivered and shook with excitement and moaned deep in her throat, clutching helplessly at him for support. And then her dark lashes lifted and over his bent shoulder she

focused on a tiny ice-blue handbag sitting like an unex-
ploded bomb on a nearby table.

'Your mother's left her handbag behind!' she gasped
strickenly.

Santino abandoned his erotic assault on the molten
responsive heat he was engaged in exploring and slowly,
very slowly lifted his dark head again. His eyes were as
blank and uncomprehending as the blacked-out windows
of his parents' limousine.

'Her bag...over there!' Frankie raised a shaking hand
to point at the offending article. 'She could walk back
in here again at any minute!'

Santino's lush black lashes swept down and then up
again. He focused on her and his fingers slowly, reluctantly loosened their grip on her dress to let the hem fall
again. He snatched in a shuddering breath, dark colour
igniting over the taut slant of his superb cheekbones.

Frankie trembled, embarrassed by what she had almost allowed to happen between them. 'Maybe we
should go upstairs,' she muttered unevenly.

Santino stepped reluctantly back. The silence
hummed. She opened the door with a fumbling hand and
finally worked up the courage to turn her head and look
at him again. In a driven motion he looped a punitive
hand into her tumbled hair and took her mouth with
speaking passionate brevity. As he drew away from her
again, eyes ablaze with hunger, his breathing audibly
fractured, she very nearly snatched him back into her
arms.

All of a quiver, she started walking across the hall and
up the spectacular staircase. A masculine hand closed
possessively, impatiently over her clenched fingers. On
the semi-circular landing, she stole a glance at him. It
was a mistake...or *was* it? For it was a mistake that
made Santino reveal the strength of his own desire all
over again. He succumbed to the apparent temptation
and encouragement of that one little glance by closing

his arms round her so tightly she could barely breathe, crushing her to him and kissing her until her head swam. The merest persistence might well have persuaded her that there was nothing remotely wrong with making love in a corridor.

But he jerked back from her then with a growling sound of frustration. 'Only this morning you were a virgin. I should be making allowances for that...I'm not.'

She met burning golden eyes and knew she was utterly enslaved.

'I want you so much I am in agony,' Santino gritted unevenly.

Incapable of speech, she nodded like a submissive marionette.

In silence, he snatched her up into his powerful arms and strode at speed down the corridor. He set her down in a bedroom but she had no time to absorb the newness of her surroundings. Santino was unzipping her dress, tugging it down her arms, releasing the front catch on her bra, and, without even waiting for either garment to drop away, he brought up his hands to hungrily enclose the pouting swell of her bare breasts.

She caught their reflection in a tall cheval-glass as she strained helplessly back into the hard, virile heat of his powerful physique. As he massaged her achingly responsive flesh and played with the throbbing pink buds desperate for his attention, she looked wanton, abandoned. And even as she writhed in tormented pleasure she stared, watching his dark, passionately intent face above hers, learning for the first time that she had power too, the power to make Santino crave her like a drug—the power to make him *need* her...?

Intoxicated by that knowledge, she twisted round in his arms and blindly sought his sensual mouth again for herself. His tongue stabbed between her lips, flicked over her tender palate and drove her wild. As her knees sagged she clung to him, and he tumbled her down on

the bed behind her, following her there without once
freeing her swollen mouth.

'*Per amor di Dio*…you're a witch…this isn't how it
was supposed to be!' As Santino wrenched her from the
folds of the dress still crumpled round her waist, Frankie
flinched from that snarling intonation. Stunning dark
eyes alight with splintering hostility clashed with hers.
And then, insane even as it seemed to her in that split
second of stark confusion, he kissed her again with the
kind of drowning erotic thoroughness that plunged her
back into sensual oblivion.

Impatiently dispensing with the silky panties which
still clung to her slender hips, Santino wasted no time
in rediscovering the unbearably hot, moist welcome
awaiting him. With an exultant growl, he pushed back
her thighs and came over her like a conqueror to thrust
with urgent, forceful hunger into the heart of her yielding
body.

Frankie cried out, her spine arching on a relentless
surge of excitement. He was wild for her and she was
hopelessly out of control. For tormenting minutes of terrifyingly intense pleasure, he drove her ruthlessly to satisfaction. The explosive, blinding shock waves of climax
hurtled through every fibre of her being and totally
wiped her out.

The first thing she noticed after that was the speed
with which Santino jerked away from her. A sudden chill
cooled her bare damp skin and she was filled with a
devastating sense of disorientation and loss, because
what she craved at that instant was for him to hold her
tight. Then the screaming silence registered. Slowly she
opened her eyes on an unfamiliar ceiling. Her gaze crept
almost fearfully down the walls and found Santino. Disturbingly, he was still fully dressed.

He moved back to the foot of the bed, where she was
spread out like a recently plundered human sacrifice. She
was in shock, ravaged by the primal hunger of his pos-

session. Santino was strikingly pale beneath his naturally golden skin. In that awful silence he stared down at her as if he wasn't quite sure how she had got there, or indeed who had brought her to such a state. And then those beautiful dark eyes filled with a mortifying mix of stark regret and compassion.

In an impatient movement, he snatched up a silk-fringed throw from a nearby chair and covered her shivering body with it. But out of sight was very obviously not out of mind. Dense black lashes screening his gaze, Santino breathed raggedly, 'I'll run a bath for you.'

He got about twelve feet away before Frankie unglued her tongue from the roof of her mouth to mutter chokily, 'Why don't you try drowning yourself in it?'

Rolling onto her side, she curled up into a tight ball. All of a sudden she felt like a whore he had picked up and now wanted to throw out. He was ashamed of himself, so therefore she had to be ashamed of herself too. Where had she ever got the stupid idea that his physical desire for her body could be a cause for celebration?

'I'm starting to feel like a split personality,' Santino confessed in an abrupt and charged undertone. 'I have never before fallen on a woman like a ravening beast...'

Nor had his ego rejoiced in the force of his own rapacious sexual hunger for her, she recalled numbly.

'I know you enjoyed it, but—'

At that undiplomatic reminder, Frankie reared up to face him again. 'Get out of here!' she screamed at him full blast.

Santino surveyed her in frustration and fanned out his long fingers in eloquent emphasis. 'That won't solve anything...and it would make me feel worse.'

'*Good!*' Frankie shot back, tears erupting without warning to pour down her cheeks.

On familiar ground with that development, Santino dropped down beside her and framed her distraught face between inexpressibly gentle hands. His vibrantly handsome features were stamped with remorse. 'I wanted to punish you…I really did want to punish you. But when I looked at you a minute ago I saw the teenager who once loved me, and you really don't look very much older now. No matter what you have done, it *was* only money and I *am* an excessively wealthy man,' he conceded grimly. 'But I wish I could go back to that day in the café at La Rocca and freeze time—'

'Y-yes,' Frankie stammered, shaken that the exact same thought which had occurred to her should now be occurring to him.

Santino's eloquent mouth quirked. 'Although, to be honest, I'm not sure it would've helped. It was your lies which enraged me most. I have a terrible temper. I'm not a very forgiving person…yet somehow all that anger has suddenly drained out of me. So I was disappointed in you, *deeply* disappointed…' He still felt the need to stress that, but a broad shoulder shifted in a fatalistic shrug of acceptance.

'But what if I wasn't really guilty of having taken all that money?' Frankie muttered in an impulsive rush. Having been hanging off his every word, she was on the very brink of confessing the truth, because it really hurt that he should still think of her as a liar, a cheat and a thief. Indeed all she needed to prompt her into telling all was a little sympathetic encouragement. 'S-suppose…I mean, suppose I was just trying to protect Mum?'

As he listened, Santino's lean face hardened and darkened again like a threatening thundercloud. 'Don't be childish, Francesca. You can't magically remake my image of you by taking refuge behind *more* lies,' he warned her with harsh impatience, misreading her motivation in having asked such loaded questions.

'I know, but I—'

'Listen to me,' Santino cut in with warning gravity. 'If it wasn't for your involvement in that financial deception, I'd have had your precious mother charged with fraud and banged up in custody by now! Believe me, it goes very much against the grain to let her escape that punishment, but I can't put her in the dock without putting *you* right up there beside her.'

Registering that her lie—her false confession of having deliberately conspired with Della to defraud him—was the only thing that appeared to stand between her mother and a probable prison sentence, Frankie dropped her eyes fearfully again and pinned her tremulous mouth shut, grateful she hadn't said enough to arouse any real suspicion that she might not be guilty as charged. It was dauntingly obvious to her that Santino, assured of her own lack of complicity in the crime, would without hesitation go ahead and prosecute her dishonest parent.

'Wise decision.' Santino complimented her on her silence. 'You have to face up to what you did…but that doesn't mean that you can't change.'

Ducking free of his hold and rubbing at her swollen eyes, she sighed heavily. 'I guess not…'

'You're still my wife and I am responsible for your well-being,' Santino continued more gently. 'That definitely shouldn't encompass reducing you to a sobbing heap on my bed. I should've controlled my desire for you.'

'Yes… I mean, *no*… I—' Meeting the questioning look in Santino's clear, frighteningly intelligent gaze, Frankie shrank and lowered her eyes again, terrified of revealing too much. What had provoked her distress was his apparent rejection of her in the aftermath of that shatteringly intense bout of intimacy.

'I imagine you're rather sore,' Santino murmured ruefully. 'And sex should always be equally pleasurable for both partners. I should never have put my need ahead of your capacity for enjoyment.'

'Stop talking down to me,' Frankie urged in growing embarrassment. 'I knew what I was doing too.'

'But you don't...that's the trouble—that's the prob-
lem,' Santino contradicted her almost fiercely, slapping
down her challenge before it could even get off the
ground. 'You just do what you feel like doing at any
given moment. I swear that in all your life you've never
looked more than thirty seconds forward into the future!
And that recklessness is like a contagious disease that
has spread to afflict me as well...but with me it stops,
here and now!'

Having delivered that character assessment with the
speaking incredulity and censure of a male who regarded
her impulsive spontaneity as a highly dangerous weakness likely to lead to dire consequences, he sprang fluidly upright and strode away from her with determination. 'I'll run you a bath and have an evening meal sent
up. You must be hungry...I know I am.'

Frankie scrambled off the bed, secured the vibrant
blue throw with a knot above her breasts and hurried
across the room to lodge herself in the doorway of the
breathtakingly luxurious bathroom. She watched him
turning on the gold taps above a big oval-shaped tub and
his every measured graceful movement enthralled her.
Indeed every facet of Santino enthralled her quite unashamedly now that she had admitted to herself that she
was still head over heels in love with him.

Had that gorgeous black hair always flopped over his
brow like silk when he bent down? Did any other male
possess such wondrously shapely and erotically assured
hands? She felt the deep, intimate ache of his possession
with instinctive pride. Whether he had liked it or not,
Santino *had* needed her, and similiarly, it seemed,
Santino *could* be passion's slave.

So he wasn't exactly happy about that reality just at
this moment, but that wild bout of lovemaking had acted
like some sort of catharsis on him. That chilling anger
and detachment had gone. She had the Santino she remembered back and, dear heaven, he was so perfect it

was all she could do to restrain herself from hurling herself ecstatically into his arms. He could be so tender, so caring. There he was, running a bath for her. He had even admitted himself to have been in the wrong. So many men found that impossible.

She really had picked a winner at sixteen. If only she could make him feel the same way *this* time...if only she could make him fall in love with her within the space of three weeks. Please, God, she prayed, fervently promising that if she got to hang onto Santino she would try never to ask for divine intervention again.

Santino straightened to find himself the sole focus of her utterly mesmerised attention. Slight colour burnished his superb cheekbones, stunning dark eyes veiling fast. 'Don't look at me like that,' he breathed very, very quietly.

'Like what?' Frankie was dizzy with the overpowering strength of her emotions and the amount of restraint it took to keep her distance from him.

Santino expelled his breath in a stark hiss. 'Having a good time in bed doesn't naturally mean that I love you or that you love me, *piccola mia*...'

Even softly voiced, and couched with that old endearment, the message still went home with the force of an axe attack on a vulnerable target. Frankie went white. Her gaze slewed to the water shimmering in the depths of the tub. 'I know that,' she tried to say with a light, dismissive laugh, but somewhere between her throat and her lips the laugh got horribly strangled and emerged like a discordant squeak.

'Right now, you don't know what you're feeling,' Santino informed her arrogantly. 'A long time ago you were infatuated with me...and now I've become your very first lover—'

'There was no stopping you!' Frankie reminded him helplessly.

'But if I had known you were a virgin, if you had

been honest with me, Francesca…I would never have touched you,' Santino countered with that brand of deadly sincerity that struck like a cobra when it was least welcome. 'When I believed that you were experienced, demanding the wedding night I had never had did not seem such a big deal.'

Frankie crossed her arms in a jagged motion, tucking shaking hands out of sight. 'No big deal…oh?' Even to her own ears, her voice sounded unnaturally shrill, which wasn't surprising when she felt as if she was dying by inches with every word he spoke.

'Possibly that wasn't the best choice of words,' Santino conceded, his hard jawline clenching. 'But you did go out of your way to convince me that you had had other lovers… Francesca, this really isn't a conversation I want to have with you right now. I think what we both need is a little breathing space from each other.'

That news could only devastate her. She could feel her brittle control over her tumultous emotions breaking up. 'I see…yes, I really *do* see—in spite of my lack of sexual sophistication. You're the kind of creep who has one-night stands and vanishes like Scotch mist before dawn!'

'How would you know? *Dio mio*…you've never had anyone else to compare me with!' Santino launched at her rawly.

Frankie's spine was planted so hard up against the tiled wall, she was convinced she would bear the impressions of the lines of grouting for the rest of her life, but she couldn't have stayed upright without that support.

Santino slowly shook his darkly handsome head and rested steady dark eyes on her. 'And possibly I'm not sorry to know that… But what I'm trying to say is that—'

'You've come to your senses now…and you've had what you wanted, so get lost?' Frankie slotted in with distaste and pain. 'There, I've said it for you and saved you the trouble of saying anything!'

At that assurance, Santino's facial muscles tensed with fierce anger. He raised his arms high in a movement that fully illustrated his wrathful impatience and dropped them again. Scorching dark golden eyes struck hers. 'You're so bloody melodramatic! Listen to yourself,' he grated. 'How the hell could I say such things or even *think* them? Not only are you my wife, you might even be pregnant with my child!'

'Oh, not *that* again.' Frankie studied her bare pink toes as they tried to curl like strained claws into the immaculate tiled floor. It stopped her whole body from drooping. It stopped her lashing out at him in an agony of pain for telling her yet more that she didn't want to hear.

'Can you tell me it isn't an even greater possibility now? *Santo cielo*...I couldn't even wait long enough to get my clothes off; do you think I had the presence of mind to protect you?' Santino demanded rawly.

'I want my bath,' Frankie announced, staring at the tub as if it might yet provide an escape hatch to another world, because it was devastatingly clear that Santino just could not wait to escape from her. 'And then I'm going home to London where I intend to go for the fastest divorce on record.'

Temper in check again, Santino dealt her a fulminating look. 'You will go nowhere. I'll use my city apartment for a couple of days. As I pointed out, neither of us is sufficiently grounded in calm or reality at this moment to be rational.'

Frankie had already turned away. 'Just go, then!' she urged him feverishly.

'Look at me...'

'I don't want to...I just want to be alone now—'

Santino strode forward and curved strong hands over

her rigid shoulders. 'I can't leave you feeling like this, *cara*.'

Frankie yanked herself free of his hold and stalked away from him. 'Stop treating me like some overgrown helpless child. I may be much more emotional than you are but I *am* an adult!'

'You don't always behave like one.'

Frankie spun in outrage and found Santino still far too close for comfort. Planting her hands on his broad chest, she gave him an aggressive shove away from her. As the backs of his legs collided with the low rim of the tub, he uttered a startled growl and overbalanced. He fell backwards into the water with a huge splash.

Stunned, Frankie simply stared, and then hysterical giggles clogged up her throat. Santino flung her a look of seething black fury, planted two powerful hands on the ceramic edge and launched himself back onto the tiled floor. 'If you were a man, I would knock you through that wall for that!' he roared at her full blast.

Frankie covered her convulsing mouth. His suit was plastered to him like a second skin and the floor was flooded. In hauling himself out with such force he appeared to have brought half the bathwater with him. 'It was an accident,' she breathed shakily. 'It really was. I didn't mean for you to fall in—'

'I am *out* of here!' Santino raked with the slashing emphasis of one forceful brown hand. 'And I will not be back until you convince me that you can behave like a grown-up!'

The grown-up without the sense of humour stalked dripping from the bathroom, slammed the door on her, slammed the door on the bedroom... And Frankie? Frankie soaked all the towels mopping up the water and dully appreciated that Santino wasn't perfect after all. He hadn't been joking about that temper. And, sitting there on the floor in lonely silence, she was too shell-shocked by that old, horribly familiar sense of agonised rejection to even begin to move beyond that stage.

CHAPTER TEN

FRANKIE reached several conclusions within the following thirty-six hours. She paced the floor and cried and slept in frenetic bouts without once leaving Santino's spacious bedroom suite.

Infuriatingly, she was constantly interrupted by the almost continuous proffering of healthy meals, regular snacks and drinks brought by the household staff. Acquainted with her habit of holing up to brood, and doubtless cruelly aware that it might be difficult to grieve with proper passion when one had to keep on opening the door to face other people, Santino had evidently left instructions that she was to be fed and watered on the hour, every hour. She was wholly unappreciative of being physically deserted but having her 'well-being' controlled from a convenient distance.

She had found Hamish, her childhood teddy, seated on an open shelf in Santino's dressing room. He was sadly tatty but he still wore his tartan scarf. She hugged the old toy to her as if he was her best friend. She acquainted herself with every single item of clothing Santino kept at the Villa Fontana and was not once tempted to slash anything to shreds.

Santino was gone. She was miserable, bereft, tormented by loss and loneliness. The light had gone out of her life. She knew it was melodramatic to feel like that, but that was how she felt and there wasn't much she could do about it. In the grip of her emotional high she was wretchedly aware that she had made some very foolish assumptions. Santino had offered her three weeks and it looked as if one shattering day had been more than enough to satisfy him. Her swansong, she thought painfully, and an insultingly brief one.

His sole reason for wanting her to remain here in Italy for the present appeared to relate to his fear that he might have fathered a child on her. Presumably, when she was able to reassure him on that point, he would be happy for her to leave. She refused to think of the possibility that she might not be able to give him that reassurance. She was wretched enough without subjecting herself to the imagined horrors of finding herself pregnant by a male who didn't want to be her husband and who certainly didn't want to be saddled with the burden of an inconveniently fertile wife he was keen to divorce.

No, Santino didn't love her and obviously he never, ever would, because, heaven knew, if he'd been even slightly susceptible he should've fallen in love with her a long time ago. Clearly he saw her as obsessive and excessive. He was her opposite in every way. Intellectual, self-disciplined, coldly logical when challenged and emotionally reserved...at least in the love department...but he could just about cope with 'fond', she conceded grudgingly.

When Santino did marry again, it would probably be to someone like that blonde she had seen him with in Cagliari five years ago. A classically lovely woman, elegant and poised, around his age and therefore well past the stage of immature urges and inappropriate behaviour.

Someone who would smile sweetly when he got patronising, controlling or domineering. Someone who would let him have the last word. Someone who would never dream of laughing when he fell in the bath in the middle of an argument. Someone equipped with the blue-blooded background necessary to become an acceptable member of the Vitale family. Santino might have told his father that the Vitales were not royalty, but for all that he lived like a king.

The first package arrived with her breakfast tray on

the second day. She pulled off the giftwrap and found herself looking at a framed cartoon of a man who had fallen into a bath. He was the very picture of injured dignity. And along the bottom, in Santino's forceful black scrawl, it said, 'As well as the temper, I confess to a tendency to take myself rather too seriously...'

For a stunned moment Frankie gaped at it. It had been a very long time since Santino had used his artistic talent to amuse her. Then she started to laugh and she got out of bed to have a shower and wash her hair.

The second package arrived mid-morning. Another cartoon featuring a bath scene, but this time with a figure that was recognisably herself starring as the victim of an accidental drenching, and she was screeching blue murder about getting her hair and her clothes soaked. Frankie wasn't quite so quick to laugh at that scenario because it forced her to admit that, had their roles been reversed, she would've been every bit as furious as he had been.

Typical Santino; he gave with one hand and slapped you down with the other. She groaned but then she smiled. After that she got dressed in a light green shift dress that she usually wore only for dressy occasions. When she heard the helicopter, she was already expecting it and planning to greet him with her brightest smile. Santino, ever the polished diplomatist, had smoothed over raw feelings with innate charm. Even at a distance he manipulated her, but possibly on this occasion, when she did feel out of her depth, it was for the best. All she had left now was her pride and the inner prayer that she could now be as casual and cool as he would be.

She was waiting in the hall when Santino strode into the villa. Clad in a lightweight beige suit of sensational cut, complemented by a white shirt and a burgundy silk tie, he stole the very breath from her lungs. It was as if thirty-six hours without Santino had dimmed her memory and, seeing him again in the flesh, she was simply bowled over by his dramatic dark good looks, his commanding height and fantastic build. She just stared, utterly appalled by the huge, unstoppable wave of love and lust that washed over her.

'I missed you,' Santino admitted, running brilliant dark-shadowed eyes over her stiff, defensive face. 'I *really* missed you.'

Even though it was a little late for the greeting speech she had planned, because he had got in first, Frankie's mind was now so blank she still seized on that speech in desperation. 'I bet your heart sank when you saw me standing here waiting like some pantomime wife hovering eagerly for hubby's return,' she reeled off at accelerated speed and with a frantically wide smile. 'But I thought, in the circumstances, it would be kind of funny—'

'Funny?' Santino's initial smile was beginning to freeze slightly round the edges.

'Like black joke funny?' Frankie pressed brightly. 'Because I don't know about you but I'm so relieved we're back to being just friends again. You have to admit that we really couldn't connect on any other level because we've got nothing in common…except the bed thing—and that was really only mutual curiosity that sparked a couple of fun encounters. You know…not something anybody adult would take seriously.'

Santino strolled round behind her and her brows pleated as she began to turn to see what he was doing. 'What are you—?'

'I was just looking to see if there was a key in your back,' Santino confided drily. 'And then possibly I could switch you off because you are thumping with great tactless hobnailed boots over some very sensitive areas and I've only been home for thirty seconds.'

Frankie swallowed convulsively.

'Maybe if I walk outside again and we run this scene

afresh you could do the pantomime wife thing,' Santino
suggested flatly.

'What do you want from me?' Frankie wailed then.

'I just want you to be you.'

'I don't understand...' she muttered.

Santino closed a long arm round her painfully taut
shoulders and slowly walked her through the double
doors that opened out into the loggia which ran along
the rear of the villa. 'It's not important, *cara*. The fault
is entirely mine. I shouldn't have left you alone for so
long.'

Every treacherously susceptible sense urged Frankie
to snuggle into that arm like a purring cat, but she
wouldn't even let the back of her head brush against his
shoulder. 'Actually, I appreciated the time alone...and
your cartoons made me laugh...but I really just want to
get back to my own life now...OK?'

'No, that's out of the question,' Santino said instantaneously.

'Why on earth should it be?' Withdrawing hurriedly
from the shelter of his arm, Frankie glanced up at him,
but she learnt nothing from the nonchalant calm stamped
on that lean, strong face. She walked from the shaded
loggia with its comfortable seating areas into the beautiful secluded gardens. There she came to a halt in front
of a softly playing fountain.

'You're thinking about the pregnancy thing again,
aren't you?' she muttered finally.

Santino dealt her a rueful smile. 'As opposed to the
bed thing?'

'Be serious...' She was struggling to barricade her
heart from the stunning effect of a casual smile which
could send threatening shock waves of response through
her. 'It's highly unlikely that we'll be unlucky.'

'That depends on your interpretation of lucky. When
will you know?' Santino enquired lazily.

She tensed and shrugged. Teresa's prudish attitude to

all bodily functions had left its mark during Frankie's adolescence. 'Sooner or later...but don't ask me how soon or how late because I'm not sure.'

As that particular brief monthly event had never interfered in the slightest with Frankie's routine, she didn't bother to keep a note of dates and could only dimly recall that the last one had been two or three weeks earlier.

'We're not short of time,' Santino responded with staggering cool. 'And it's pointless to worry about something we have no influence over.'

'You've certainly changed your tune.'

'Maybe I've warmed up to the idea of being a father...maybe I might even be disappointed if you aren't pregnant,' Santino murmured rather tautly.

That amazing suggestion left Frankie with a dropped jaw. She spun away, feverishly striving to work out what good reason he could have to say such a thing. And then the proverbial penny dropped. 'You don't believe in abortion, do you?'

Right there in front of her, Santino froze. 'Surely you weren't thinking along those lines?'

She shook her head, fascinated by his inability to conceal his relief. Then her own face fell. Now she knew *why* he was being so sincere and pleasant. He was intent on improving relations between them in advance of them finding out. Very practical and sensible, she thought, loathing him for his foresight. Whatever happened, they would still get a divorce. He had made that clear from the outset, hadn't he? But gaining access to any child might be problematic if he was on bad terms with his ex-wife.

Santino smiled and she wasn't surprised. Nudged in the right direction, she seemed to have obediently served up the responses he wanted. 'I suggest we seal our new understanding by having lunch.'

And fifteen minutes later they did exactly that. A light

and delicious meal was served informally in the shade of the loggia. They had only just sat down when a marmalade cat, tail held high, strolled towards them. 'Topsy...' Frankie whispered, and instantly thrust her chair back to get down on her knees to welcome her former pet. 'Gosh, she's looking well!'

'Pudding's probably asleep on the window seat in my study. He doesn't hunt much now...he's getting too old,' Santino reminded her gently as he absorbed her uninhibited delight in the reunion.

'You didn't use to approve of pets indoors.'

'The staff pamper the pair of them. They are extremely spoilt cats. I didn't have much choice,' Santino told her, modestly downplaying his role while Topsy wrapped herself sinuously round his ankles, purring like an engine and clearly demonstrating her affection.

Smiling, Frankie returned to the table.

'By the way...I've signed those villas over for rental to your business partner,' Santino advanced, startling her. 'However, I suspect that you would still find it difficult to work with Matt Finlay again.'

'But why?'

'He's a bad loser. He'll hold a grudge because you dented his ego—'

'Matt and I are good friends...'

'Good friends don't tell crude lies about each other,' Santino responded drily.

The reminder made Frankie redden. 'A couple of months ago, he started trying to change our relationship,' she confided ruefully. 'Suddenly he was acting as if he was attracted to me when he never had been before. And then at the farmhouse he said that marrying me would've made good business sense...'

'A wife with money of her own would appeal to an ambitious man, particularly when the agency's income had dropped and he was having to tighten his belt.'

She almost opened her mouth to tell him that Matt

had never been under the impression that she had further funds to dip into after she had bought into the business, but then she remembered that Matt had commented more than once on her mother's wealthy lifestyle. He might easily have assumed that marrying Della's daughter would ultimately prove to be well worth his while.

'How *could* Matt be that calculating?' Frankie whispered sickly.

Santino was now studying her intently, hooded dark eyes not missing a single expression that crossed her shaken and hurt face.

'It's so upsetting to think of someone I liked and trusted looking on me as a potential piggybank. And it's so horribly two-faced when all the time Matt was behaving as if it was me he wanted…to think I even worried about hurting his feelings!' Grimacing, Frankie looked at Santino, wondering when and why he had gone so unusually quiet.

Spiky black lashes fanned low on lustrous dark eyes and his shapely mouth slanted into a sudden wolfish smile. 'Horribly two-faced,' Santino agreed obediently.

Frankie belatedly registered that she had completely forgotten that she herself had confessed to having spent five years ripping off Santino for every penny she could get. Her fair skin burned and she didn't know where to put herself or where to look.

Santino stretched a casual hand across the table and briefly enclosed her rigidly knotted fingers. 'Let's talk about something more entertaining,' he suggested lightly. 'How would you like to spend the next few weeks?'

She was intensely relieved by the change of subject. Extraordinary as it seemed to her, Santino didn't appear to have twinned her apparent dishonesty with Matt's.

'How?' A look of dreamy abstraction slowly covered her face. 'I'd love to do Rome…ancient Rome, I mean… The Forum, the Colosseum, the Basilica, the

Pantheon…all the places I read about when I took ancient history classes.' Then she frowned, thinking about all the publicity the news of their marriage had received. 'Will we be able to go out and about freely?'

'The paparazzi still think we're in Sardinia, and there are many other ways of avoiding them,' Santino informed her with wry amusement. 'In this instance, I think the wisest move would be to simply release a photograph of us together. That's really what they all want. Once that is released, it won't be worth their while to chase after us with the same fervour.'

That afternoon, Santino showed her round the estate. Since it was very large, and Santino demonstrated a surprising eagerness to introduce her to every member of staff and every tenant who crossed their path, they didn't actually get back to the villa until dinnertime. After their evening meal, he treated her to a tour of the house. Starting at the present day and working backwards in history, he entertained her with fascinating stories about the lives and loves of the previous occupants.

The Villa Fontana had been built to house the flamboyant but much loved mistress of a rich aristocrat.

'They had seven children together…those soulful little cherubs have their faces.' Santino indicated the beautiful frescos on the walls. 'He married her after the birth of their first child. He was an aristocrat and she was a peasant's daughter—'

'That sounds like the opening to a sleazy joke,' Frankie could not resist saying. After exposure to his mother's snobbery, she was supersensitive to any reference either to the existence of a class divide or that word 'mistress'.

Santino's dark eyes stabbed into her with unexpected force. 'Whatever they didn't appear to have in common kept them together for well over thirty years!'

'If that voluptuous blonde is a faithful representation of the lady, we know very well what kept her lover hooked. She looks like a raving sexpot,' Frankie opined thinly, blondes being a no more welcome subject. 'And she paid for it, didn't she? *Seven* kids in the days when women often died giving birth and there was no pain relief…he was a selfish pig!'

'I don't believe I have ever regarded their lifelong love in that light before,' Santino confessed with sudden intense amusement.

'Probably not…but then you're a man, aren't you? She traded sex for security. If a woman was poor she didn't have much else to trade in those days, and I bet her family practically sold her to him…although I have to admit that he's not bad-looking,' Frankie conceded, studying the gentleman in question. 'He was a good bit older, though, wasn't he?'

'About ten years older,' Santino supplied, his amusement ebbing.

'So she had the generation gap to deal with as well.'

Santino tensed. 'Is that how you feel with me?'

Taken aback by his personal reaction to her facetious comment, Frankie wriggled like a guppy being reeled in. 'You're only twenty-nine, Santino—'

'Take your foot out of your mouth and tell me truthfully,' Santino gritted, suddenly demonstrating his recent extreme volatility for a usually even-tempered male by backing her up against a pillar. '*Do* you feel a generation gap with me?'

Shaken and confused, she sighed, 'Santino…to me, you're just you.'

A surprisingly understanding smile drove the tension from his lean face. 'Not like anyone else?'

Urgently she nodded in agreement. 'Unique,' she added, and then, feeling inexplicably exposed beneath the onslaught of those shrewd golden eyes, she lowered her head. 'I'm really tired,' she muttered. 'I think it's time I went to bed.'

There was a stark little silence and then Santino withdrew a step.

Naturally they wouldn't be sharing a bed any more, and she wanted to clear her stuff out of his room before he went up to bed later. The less she reminded him of their brief intimacy, the more he would relax with her, wouldn't he? And she wanted him to relax; she really did. If this next couple of weeks was all the time they were ever to spend together, she wanted to make the most of it.

Frankie had just got into bed in a room across the landing when Santino strode in. With a start, she sat up again. Santino wore only a bathtowel, anchored precariously round his lean brown hips, and he looked really mad. Without a word, he plucked her out of bed and carried her back to his room.

'What are you doing?' she gasped. 'Now that we're being friends again, we *can't* sleep together!'

'I don't want another friend. I've got plenty of friends. I want you in my bed, where you belong.' Santino punctuated that announcement by settling her between the sheets, casting aside his towel and sliding in beside her. 'For the moment, that will suffice. *Buona notte, cara.*'

Shellshocked, Frankie lay there in the darkness. 'But we're on the brink of a divorce; *why?*'

'If you're really lucky these old bones of mine might give out first and you'll find yourself a very merry and extremely rich widow instead,' Santino countered sardonically from the far side of the bed. '*Madre di Dio*…is it wise for me to put ideas of that nature into your head?'

'Don't you dare say things like that even as a joke!' It was an appalled and superstitious wail of censure. 'I'd *die* if anything happened to you!'

And as soon as those words escaped Frankie she clamped a horrified hand to her open mouth.

'That sounds just a little extreme to me,' Santino countered with an incredulous derision that was hugely painful for her to hear. 'And completely unbelievable coming from a woman who lies, cheats and steals from me for five long years without once succumbing to an attack of conscience—'

'But I *didn't*...it was—'

'*Della*, the mother-in-law from hell,' Santino slotted in, his deep, dark drawl ringing with sizzling self-satisfaction.

Sitting up, he turned the bedside lamps back on and surveyed her with wry amusement. 'Don't you feel better having got that off your chest? I'm sorry I had to get nasty...well, so theatrical, but I know the right imaginative buttons to push with you, *cara*. Death and disloyalty, an unbeatable combination.'

'Oh, no...' Frankie moaned in horror at what she had let slip, aghast on her mother's behalf.

'You told me yourself over lunch,' Santino informed her gently. 'While you were wittering on with such enormous hurt about Finlay's dishonest intentions, it finally sunk in on me that there was no way in this lifetime that you would behave in a similiar fashion. And when were you ever able to keep secrets from me? You look so shifty and guilty when you're lying, a child could find you out. If I hadn't been in such a rage that day, I'd have seen that for myself.'

'Mum?' Frankie muttered shakily, barely able to absorb what he was telling her because he sounded so disorientatingly light-hearted.

'You should've known that there wasn't the slightest chance that I would prosecute her. Put Della in an open court to star in a sensational trial?' Santino chided incredulously. 'I would not expose you or my family to that experience merely to punish her.'

Still welded to the mattress by shock, Frankie whispered weakly, 'You mean, you *never* planned to—'

'Never.'

'But I *believed* you...you scared me out of my wits!'

Santino shot her a languorous smile, rather like a big predatory cat receiving a very welcome stroking of the ego. 'Didn't I just?'

Frankie shot across the big bed like an electric eel. 'How could you *do* that to me?' she raked at him furiously.

'At the time, with pleasure,' Santino admitted. 'After all, while you were industriously protecting a woman who could single-handedly gut a shoal of piranha fish and emerge unscathed from the bloodbath, it never once occurred to you to consider me—'

'*You?*' Frankie echoed in a tone that shook with rage after that highly offensive reference to her mother.

Santino snaked out his arms and entrapped her as she leant over him. 'Think hard,' he advised with mocking dark eyes that flared gold as they roamed over her lovely face. 'It would help me along tremendously. Poor, unfortunate Santino, evidently saddled with a wife who is an unashamed criminal…and who is also potentially pregnant. Nightmare street.'

'But I'm not an unashamed criminal,' she mumbled rather unsteadily as he drew her down, crushing her breasts intimately into the hard wall of his hair-roughened chest.

'Hmm…' Santino sighed throatily, angling his powerful hips up into thrusting contact with her slight, trembling length and introducing her to the hungry, aroused thrust of his manhood.

'No, Santino…the divorce,' Frankie reminded him breathlessly.

Santino rested his arrogant dark head back on the pillows and studied her with deceptively sleepy golden eyes. 'This intense preoccupation with divorce is beginning to worry me. I am only three days into the three weeks you signed up for. What's an extra fun encounter here and there…between friends?' he enquired with husky persuasion.

'No...' Hot in places she was too ashamed to acknowledge, Frankie gave him a look of pleading reproach even as her slender thighs somehow drifted slightly apart and she found herself inexplicably rubbing her quivering body with helpless enticement against his.

'Once again...louder and with real commitment,' Santino encouraged raggedly.

'Santino...*please*...' Frankie moaned.

'No, I'm completely impartial on this,' Santino insisted stubbornly, his palms pressing her hips down on him in the most tormentingly exciting way and lingering to ease up the nightdress inch by suggestive inch and then stop dead. 'Friendship means that you have to ask to be ravished within an inch of your life. I wouldn't want to risk overstepping my boundaries. Only a husband would be confident enough of his reception to proceed without a clear invitation.'

'Santino...you *are* my husband!' Frankie practically sobbed in her frustration.

Instantaneously Santino arched up and let the tip of his tongue sensually trace the tremulous line of her generous mouth. 'You are such a fast learner, *signora*...you take my breath away...'

'Just think...' Frankie breathed headily two weeks later. 'This was *the* place to be buried in 28 BC.'

'Just think.' Santino surveyed the Mausoleum of Augustus, a rather undistinguished mound covered with weeds. He wore the look of a male striving against all the odds to rise above prosaic first impressions.

'You've got to use your imagination,' Frankie scolded.

'You've got enough for both of us, *piccola mia*.' Santino sent her a winging smile full of megawatt charm and appreciation. 'You have taught me to view this city of mine through new eyes.'

Frankie swiftly looked away from him, heart banging

fit to burst with suppressed excitement, but as he moved fluidly closer she wandered away, pretending to be absorbed in her guidebook. By being elusive during daylight she protected herself. Everything that went on at night in bed she kept in a separate compartment. Wonderful entertaining days, endless erotic nights. It was almost like a honeymoon, she reflected with a stark pang of pain, but in her heart of hearts she knew that Santino was merely engaged in hedging all his bets.

What else could he be up to? He had been so certain she would be pregnant. Admittedly, he hadn't once mentioned that subject again, but his behaviour had helped her to work out for herself that if she did turn out to be carrying his baby there would be no divorce. Now that he knew she hadn't stolen from him, if she did prove to be pregnant, Santino would make the best of things. After all, he was *fond* of her. But suppose she wasn't pregnant? It was ironic that what she had once feared she now badly wanted to happen.

A top society photographer, who was a personal friend of Santino's, had come to the Villa Fontana to record their togetherness for posterity, and one picture had been released to a very gushy glossy international magazine without any accompanying interview. In advance of that event, Frankie had been surprised to find herself presented with a new wedding ring and a gorgeous emerald engagement ring.

'I guess I need those or we wouldn't look convincing,' she had sighed.

'I am giving you these because you are my wife,' Santino had countered levelly.

Sinking back to the present, Frankie was deeply conscious of Santino's scrutiny while she continued to finger frantically through her guidebook in search of a fresh ruin to visit.

'I think we've run out of sites,' Santino commented without a shade of irony, indeed contriving to sound deeply regretful. 'I didn't think that could be done in Rome but we have done it. Deprived of the need to tramp about like tourists from dawn to dusk, what will we do with ourselves?'

'If you've been bored, you only had to say so.'

'I don't get bored with you.'

'You've got so flattering recently…'

'But you're not listening,' Santino breathed with a slightly raw edge to his intonation.

During the drive back to the villa, Frankie tensed in dismay. A tiny little twinge had cramped low in her stomach. Instantly she knew what that sensation meant. She turned away from Santino, eyes anguished, face draining of colour. Well, now she had her answer. She *wasn't* pregnant. She ought to tell him right now, let him off the hook, but right then she hated him for hanging himself on that hook.

But she was no better, was she? Hoping to hang onto him and their marriage on the strength of a baby? That wouldn't have been right either, and she had the lesson of her own parents' marriage behind her, so she didn't even have the excuse of optimistic ignorance. Physical attraction had brought her parents together but it hadn't been enough to keep them together.

A muffled choking sound escaped her as she clambered out of the car.

'What's wrong?' Santino demanded.

'Nothing!' she cried, and ran into the villa and didn't stop running until she reached the bathroom off their bedroom and locked the door behind her.

'Francesca!' Santino rapped impatiently on the door.

'I'll be out in a minute!' she promised, struggling to face courageously up to the destruction of all her hopes.

She finally shuffled out, tear-stained and looking tragic. As yet there was no actual proof that her period had arrived, but she just *knew* there very soon would be.

In her view that one tiny twinge was utterly foolproof confirmation.

'You're not feeling well, are you? Do you think we should do a pregnancy test?' Santino asked, with an award-winning lack of tact and what she interpreted as a vastly unconvincing look of excitement and anticipation.

Reacting to that unfortunate question as if it had been a cruel and deliberate taunt, Frankie burst into great gulping sobs. 'I hate you...go away!'

Disobliging to the last in his innate belief that he always knew what was best for her, Santino lifted her up as if she were a very fragile glass ornament and laid her carefully down on the bed, slipping off her shoes. She rolled over and bawled her eyes out. 'Leave me alone!' she sobbed in between times, because he kept on trying to put his arms round her and smooth her hair and do sympathetic things that only made her feel more wretchedly guilty than ever.

Never had Frankie been more deeply ashamed of herself. She couldn't even meet his eyes now. That she had been prepared to use a baby to keep Santino made her feel like a shockingly selfish and wicked woman. It would've been so desperately unfair to him when he didn't love her. And all the love she could give him could never compensate him for being denied the opportunity to find a woman he could love.

'You really...seriously...genuinely...want me to leave you alone?' Santino prompted with astonishing persistence, crouching athletically down by the side of the bed in an effort to get a look at her tear-swollen face. 'You usually don't mean it...in fact, if I *do* go, I'm the worst in the world. You taught me that a long time ago.'

Tell him, her conscience urged, and the very words of admission formed on her lips, but unfortunately another great wail of misery forced an exit and somehow took over and she thrust her face weakly into the pillows.

'I n-need a breathing space,' she gasped in stricken defeat, borrowing heavily from his terminology.

Vaulting upright again, Santino made no response. He seemed to take a terribly long time walking to the door, but Frankie kept her head down until the door thudded softly shut on his departure.

She *had* to pull herself together before she could face discussing the end of their marriage. And what was Santino likely to think after she had treated him to such a hysterical display? Could she plead an episode of howling premenstrual tension? Dear heaven, she would tell any lie sooner than let him suspect the true source of her distress. She had worked so hard at being bright, breezy and casual. She had behaved as if they were engaged in a brief affair. Pride demanded that when she left Santino this time she would leave with her chin up high and her shoulders square.

She had known why he continued to sleep with her. He could hardly have suggested that they live in suspended animation while they waited to learn whether or not she was pregnant. Indeed every tender, caring thing Santino had done recently had simply been part of his pretence that their marriage was and could be normal. He had been fatalistically convinced that she would conceive...and he had been wrong.

Exhausted by her emotions, she decided to skip dinner. Falling into an uneasy doze, she was awakened by the phone beside the bed ringing. Still half-asleep, she snatched it up. 'I'm in Milan,' Santino's dark drawl informed her coldly.

'What are you doing there?' Frankie demanded at full incredulous volume. She had asked him for a breathing space. She had expected him to go downstairs, not transport himself to the far end of the country!

'I sense a certain contrariness in that question. What you are really saying is...how *could* you leave me?' Santino translated huskily.

'No, I just wondered…that's all,' Frankie breathed shakily, waking up enough to recall that there wasn't much point in missing him when soon she was going to be missing him every day for the rest of her life.

'I'm attending an EC banking conference.'

'That must be exciting.'

'I'll be here for two days,' Santino informed her punitively.

'*Two d—?*' Frankie bit her tongue and swallowed hard. 'Oh, how lovely for you,' she completed limply.

'I'm getting very mixed signals here. I was about to suggest that you *join*—'

'Have a really good time,' Frankie cut in chokily, before he could voice that invitation and tempt her into what would be an insane act. She snatched in a shuddering breath, despising herself for stalling on giving him the good news. Santino had every right to know that she wasn't carrying his child just as soon as it was within her power to tell him. 'Oh, y-yes, by the way,' she added flatly, 'I'm *not* pregnant.'

The answering silence pounded as noisily as her heartbeat in her eardrums.

'Isn't that just wonderful news?' Frankie gushed with tears running down her cheeks. 'I know you must be as relieved as I am. Look, we'll talk when you get back.'

She set down the cordless phone. There, it was done and she felt better for it. And telling Santino on the phone had been the best way. It had allowed them both the privacy to conceal their personal reactions. She could not have borne to see Santino's relief, not when she herself still felt so gutted by disappointment.

She now had two days to sort herself out. And it would probably take two days for her swollen face to shrink back to normal proportions. She would find out exactly when he was returning and meet him at the airport. She would be cheerful, friendly and calm. There would be no drama and no tears when they returned to the villa to discuss their divorce and the next morning she would fly back to London.

By dawn the following day, Frankie was becoming increasingly perplexed about what was going on inside her own confusing body. Her period had still not arrived. In addition, she had not experienced a single further twinge but, most unusually, her breasts were now feeling the tiniest bit tender. *What if…?* What if she had been premature in giving Santino that reassurance?

By noon of the same day, having still received no confirmation of her condition, Frankie was panicking. Santino's chauffeur, Mario, drove her into the pretty medieval town of Anguillara. Too enervated even to appreciate her lovely surroundings, Frankie purchased a pregnancy test. When the kit provided her with incontrovertible proof that she *had* conceived, she went into shock. Joy and dismay then tore at her simultaneously as she appreciated how very foolish she had been to rush into disabusing Santino of the idea that she might be pregnant. How on earth was she supposed to tell him now that she had made a mistake?

The following morning, the very day of Santino's return, Frankie began worrying that that one little cramp she had felt might be the warning of an approaching miscarriage. Appalled by the idea, already having developed powerful feelings of protectiveness towards her unborn child, she visited a busy medical practice in Bracciano. A brief examination confirmed the test results.

Then she sat feeling rather like a toddler being taught the basics while the woman doctor gently explained to her that her experience had not been unusual, nor indeed was it anything to worry about. During the earliest stages of pregnancy it was apparently quite common for a woman to misinterpret the signs that her body was giving her because it was a time of tremendous hormonal upheaval. Leaving the surgery, Frankie went shopping in a very expensive shop. She bought an elegant daffodil-yellow dress and toning shoes, her version of armour.

At three in the afternoon, Frankie arrived in the limousine at Fiumicino to meet Santino off his private jet. Of course, she could have waited until he came home, but the truth was that she just couldn't wait to see him again and gauge his reaction to the mistaken news she had given him on the phone. If he was happier than a sandboy, it would be a challenge to disenchant him.

But one thing she did know: she could not keep such news from Santino, nor could she even consider any suggestion that they should remain married for the baby's sake. It wouldn't be fair. It just would not be fair to either of them.

As Frankie watched from the VIP lounge, the jet taxied in and the steps were run up. A slim blonde woman clad in an eye-catching fuchsia-pink suit appeared first. The stewardess? No, the stewardess was still at the exit door. Santino emerged next, luxuriant black hair ruffling in the slight breeze, vibrantly handsome dark features unreadable at that distance. In odd visual conflict with his stunning, elegant appearance, he had something large and awkwardly shaped stuffed under one powerful arm.

The blonde waited at the foot of the steps for him. A bank executive? His secretary? But as Santino and the woman crossed the tarmac, drawing ever closer, their heads bent in animated conversation, Frankie began to stiffen and stare fixedly because she could not immediately accept the powerful stirrings of recognition firing danger signals from her memory banks. Her stomach gave a sick, fearful lurch, perspiration breaking out on her brow.

'Who is that woman?' she asked the chauffeur, who was standing several feet away.

The older man looked surprised by her need to ask that question. 'Melina Bucelli, *signora*.'

Frankie froze in disbelief. Simultaneously three men, seemingly springing up out of nowhere, ran across the tarmac to target Santino with their cameras. Instantly Santino's security men went into action, holding back the shouting paparazzi. Their steps quickening, Santino and his companion lifted their heads.

Frankie recognised the blonde at the same instant as Santino saw Frankie standing by the window waiting. A brilliant smile began forming on his lips and then, with the speed of light, he appeared to register what a deep, dark hole he was in and, ditching the smile for an appalled look, dropped his briefcase and the funny furry thing he was carrying and broke into a most uncool sprint, his startled security men charging in his wake.

But Santino was already too late. Breaking free of her paralysis, Frankie had raced across the VIP lounge and headed like a homing pigeon out into the mercifully crowded anonymity of the main airport building.

CHAPTER ELEVEN

FRANKIE sat staring down into her untouched cappuccino. After being forced to cope with a debilitating bout of physical sickness in a cloakroom at Fiumicino, she had finally got into a taxi and directed the driver to the city centre. She had walked the streets for what felt like miles before her trembling lower limbs had forced her to sit down at a pavement café.

Now, registering her familiar surroundings, she was ashamed to find herself in the Piazza Navona. Only last week she had been here with Santino, and undoubtedly the memory of that happy day had unerringly brought her back. Insisting that ancient sites alone were too restricting, Santino had suggested that on alternate days he would choose their destinations.

In the church of Santa Maria della Pace, he had shown her the wonderful frescos by Raphael and had linked his fingers lightly with hers. Hand in hand, like lovers, they had strolled down the Via del Governo Vecchio to admire the superb Renaissance buildings and they had lunched in a trattoria overlooking three spectacular Baroque fountains. By that stage Santino had been flirtatiously kissing her fingers one by one, mowing down her daytime defences with burnished, dark, knowing eyes that made her heart race dizzily with longing and love and need.

Frankie blinked, her mind going blank, unable to hold onto images which now filled her with such unbearable pain. She was still in deep shock. Nothing could have prepared her for the devastating discovery that the blonde kissing Santino in Cagliari five years ago and

Melina Bucelli, reputedly dear as a daughter to Sonia Vitale, were in fact one and the same woman.

Frankie had never asked Santino about the woman he had betrayed her with. She had never really wanted to know any more. In those days their marriage had been a charade. She had left that episode in the past, where it seemed to belong, never dreaming that Santino might have some ongoing relationship with the woman. Indeed she had preferred to think of that gorgeous blonde as some casual pick-up, some immoral trollop...

Yet paradoxically she could not imagine Santino choosing to become intimate with that kind of woman. And he hadn't, had he? Possessed of his aristocratic mother's stamp of approval, Melina Bucelli had to be from the same rich and privileged background. That Melina should also be exquisitely beautiful was almost too much to bear. But what continually drew Frankie to a halt in her shellshocked ruminations was a complete inability to understand the sort of relationship Santino had with the other woman.

Five years ago Santino had been Melina's lover, but he hadn't had his marriage to Frankie annulled so that he could marry the other woman. That threw up another question that Frankie could barely credit that she had never yet asked him. Why *had* Santino allowed their marriage to continue in existence for so long? Challenged, she could not come up with a single adequate explanation of why Santino had been content to remain a married man.

But then what did that matter now? Frankie asked herself dully. The night before last she had told Santino that she wasn't pregnant. She had let him off the hook and he had fairly leapt off that hook of responsibility into celebration. From that moment he had evidently considered himself free of all obligation towards Frankie. Knowing that he was now free to go ahead with a divorce, he had probably invited Melina to join him in

Milan. Naturally he wouldn't have expected Frankie to turn up to meet him at the airport. After all, in the circumstances, why should she have done such a very wifely thing?

Having stranded herself in Rome with little cash left in her purse and not the slightest idea of how to get back to the Villa Fontana by public transport, Frankie finally surrendered to hard necessity. However she felt, she had to go back to the villa to pack and she had to face Santino. After purchasing a phone card in a newspaper kiosk, she queued up to use a public phone.

She wasn't expecting Santino to answer the phone personally, and the instant he heard her hesitant voice he burst into explosive Italian, speaking too fast for her to follow. It *was* Santino and yet he didn't sound like himself. He sounded frantic, distressed, out of control.

'I want you to send a car for me...but I don't want you to be in that car,' Frankie told him in a deadened voice of exhaustion.

'Where *are* you?' Santino demanded raggedly. '*Per amor di Dio*...I've been out of my mind with worry!'

'You're really not very good at adultery, Santino...I think your life will be easier after we're divorced,' Frankie murmured flatly.

'Please tell me where you are,' Santino pressed fiercely.

She told him and added, 'If you're in the car, I won't get in,' because she couldn't face the prospect of their confrontation taking place in a confined space.

A limousine drew up in front of her less than ten minutes later. Santino's chief security man, Nardo, got out, looking very grave, and was relieved to usher her into the rear seat.

'We searched the airport over and over again,' he sighed. 'Signor Vitale was distraught at your disappearance. I was only able to persuade him to return to the villa an hour ago.'

As the door closed on her and she slumped, Frankie was surprised to find herself sharing the seat with a very large teddy bear, wearing a frilly tartan dress and, horror of horrors, carrying a miniature teddy in its arms. The teddy looked as forlorn as she felt. Her goodbye present from Milan, fully advertising Santino's apparent belief that she had no taste whatsoever and hadn't matured in the slightest. And why did the teddy have a distinctly mother-and-baby look about it? Was that supposed to be a joke he expected her to appreciate?

Obviously she was a complete fool where men were concerned. She just could not comprehend how Santino could have made passionate love to her only three nights earlier and then turned to Melina. He hadn't even paused for breath. And now she could not imagine telling him that she carried his child either...

She dozed in the car but it was like a waking dream, full of haunting slices of memory. She surfaced to find herself inside the Villa Fontana, being carried upstairs in Santino's arms. 'Put me down—'

'I thought I had lost you...I have never been so scared in my life,' Santino groaned, powerful arms tightening round her. 'Don't you ever, ever do this to me again.'

'I won't be here to do it,' she reminded him dully.

Santino settled her down in a comfortable armchair in their bedroom. Frankie studied him. He looked devastated. She had never seen a few hours make such a difference to anybody. His tie was at half-mast, half the buttons on his silk shirt were undone to reveal a brown slice of hair-roughened chest and he badly needed a shave. Beneath the stubble he was pale as death, and his eyes were haunted and dark with strain.

'You lied to me...I never thought you would do that,' Frankie confided with a jerky little laugh.

Santino frowned. 'When did I lie?'

'When I asked you who Melina was, you didn't tell me the truth.'

Santino drove long fingers roughly through his already tousled hair. 'I was thinking about Rico that day...it slipped my mind that Melina was the woman you saw me with in Cagliari five years ago—'

'*Slipped your mind?*' Frankie repeated in helpless disbelief.

'I didn't expect you to remember her... All right, I wasn't breaking my neck to raise that subject too soon. Which of us is eager to recall our more embarrassing mistakes?' Santino demanded in charged appeal. 'What you saw happen between Melina and me that day was the consequence of a moment of temptation, of weakness...and when you surprised us that was it. Nothing more happened between us, either then or since.'

'Do you seriously expect me to believe that?' Frankie whispered in despair.

'Perhaps I should have begun at the beginning. When she was eighteen, Melina was my brother's girlfriend...or his cover story, if you like,' Santino shared ruefully. 'Because Rico was gay.'

'*Gay?*' Taken by surprise, Frankie stared back at him.

'My parents could not accept him as he was. They were desperate for him to marry. They adored Melina and she adored Rico. But he never had the slightest intention of marrying her. When he died, she joined my mother in making a shrine of his memory,' Santino explained grimly. 'After a while, my mother decided that Melina would make *me* the perfect wife, but I wasn't interested. She *was*...perhaps because I look very like my late brother.'

'And that day I saw you with her in Cagliari?'

Santino tautened. 'Melina flew over to Sardinia, ostensibly to visit friends. She came to see me at the bank and I decided to take her back to my apartment for lunch. It was quite innocent until she threw herself at me in the lift...but I was not unresponsive to that invitation,' he admitted bluntly, shooting Frankie a driven look of fierce emotion. 'Had you not interrupted us, I *would* have gone to bed with her…after six months of our marriage, I was so tortured by my unsated desire for you, I would have done anything to try to kill that craving!'

Frankie was sharply disconcerted by that admission. She had never really understood, even when he had told her at the farmhouse, how hard it must have been for him to withstand the temptation to consummate their marriage. Heaven knew, she had been willing, but he had been wise to keep his distance. Then she could never have been his equal and he would swiftly have grown bored with her immature adoration.

'I would've used Melina and she deserved better. I chased after you and left her standing in the lobby that day without any explanation. It was a long time before she could forgive me for that. These days we meet solely as distant and very polite friends—'

'"Friends"…that's such an elastic term with you—'

'Melina and I met at the conference,' Santino interrupted drily. 'She has just become engaged to another banker. She flew back to Rome with me to make arrangements for a family party to announce her engagement.'

Frankie was shaken. His explanation made better sense than any other. Her suspicions vanquished, she was left feeling rather foolish and uncomfortable. 'That's going to break your mother's heart,' was all she could think to say.

'Few men marry women chosen by their mothers, *cara*.' Santino's mouth quirked. 'I should also mention that I received a rather astonishing phone call from mine this morning.'

'Oh?' Frankie had tensed.

'Surprisingly, my mother wanted to tell me how much she loved me.' Santino rested keen eyes on Frankie's betraying flush. 'She may not have shown that affection in ten years, but she was not telling me anything I didn't already know.'

'Wasn't she?' Frankie was disconcerted by that assurance.

'She has never come to terms with my brother's death, but today all of a sudden she experienced a need to contact me and say that she appreciated how very fortunate she was to have a surviving son.'

'Gosh!' Frankie exclaimed, glancing away, not wanting him to suspect her interference.

'Mamma also received the news of Melina's engagement with nothing more than a regretful sigh, and she implied that she might have been slightly hasty in saying that she would *never* accept you as a daughter-in-law. It was an amazing rapprochement.'

Silence lingered. Frankie collided tensely with clear dark golden eyes. Melina wasn't his lover, never had been his lover, or his intended wife or indeed anything else, but he hadn't even considered it important to tell her those facts. 'Why didn't you explain about Melina five years ago...why did you allow me to go on believing that you'd been unfaithful?'

'We *had* to part. You had to grow up and you couldn't do that with me,' Santino informed her tautly, watching her spin her head defensively away from him. 'To the best of my ability, I put you and our marriage to the back of my mind and got on with my life.'

'Yet you made no attempt to have our marriage annulled...'

'I didn't meet anyone else I wanted to marry. And you were a sweet memory...the woman I believed you might become figured in my mind as an ideal.'

Frankie's head swivelled instantly back to him. 'An ideal?'

Santino smiled. 'You look just like an enquiring sparrow when you do that, *cara mia*. Don't ask me to explain to you how or why I love you. I only know that I *do*...'

Her stunned eyes clung to his, her breath catching in her throat as she struggled to accept and believe in the sentiments he'd expressed with such deep and unashamed sincerity.

Santino strolled forward and reached down to grasp her hands and draw her slowly upright. Brilliant dark eyes scanned her face with immense and tender appreciation. 'We have ties that go back so many years. And you had such courage, such tremendous warmth and faith. No other woman has ever reached my heart as you did, and yet I realise now that I probably hurt you more than all the rest put together by not discouraging your attachment to me...'

Frankie leant forward into the welcoming shelter of his big, powerful body. Trembling, she rested her brow against his shoulder, eyes prickling with tears of intense happiness. 'No, I needed you then. I had nothing else,' she told him honestly. 'And being in your arms is still like coming home.'

'Today I was afraid that you weren't planning to come home again,' Santino confided unevenly, his arms closing round her slowly, as if he was still afraid to credit that the worst was over and the best was all to come. 'You switched off me so fast five years ago. Then I told myself that it was for the best, but I was scared that it could happen again...'

'I just love you more with every day,' Frankie muttered in a wobbly voice choked with tears. 'I'm really not that easy to get rid of.'

'But you are. Five years ago you severed every connection between us. You had no second thoughts. You didn't go home to face me; you just climbed on a plane. And you didn't write. I was tempted so many times to seek you out, but I knew that that wouldn't be fair. You had to be free to become an adult, and yet letting go so completely was the hardest thing I ever did.'

'I never once thought you could've felt like that.'

'I couldn't end our marriage without giving us one more chance. I had such incredibly high hopes, and the instant I saw you in La Rocca the same fierce attraction leapt into being—'

'And then Della's dishonesty got in the way.'

'But I still couldn't bear to let go of you,' Santino confided. 'I promised myself that at the end of three weeks I would be cured of you.'

'Initially I had the same objective.' Frankie carefully unknotted his tie and slipped it off. 'But it didn't work.'

'No, I just got in deeper…and deeper…and deeper…'

'You said that having a good time in bed didn't mean that you loved—'

Santino clasped a strong hand over the uncertain fingers braced against his chest. Intense dark golden eyes held hers fiercely. 'And neither it does. Even if I could never make love to you again, I would still love you.'

'But you hurt me so much saying that.'

'I didn't want you to mistake your feelings for me…I wanted you to take the time to get to know me again and be sure that what you were feeling was real and lasting. I couldn't risk you waking up some day and deciding that you were too young to be tied down and that possibly it was a mistake to have stayed married to your first lover…'

Frankie was deeply touched that Santino had suffered from his own insecurities. 'I'm sorry, but you are really the only man I have ever wanted.'

Santino coloured. 'I liked that—'

'I know…you're possessive. So am I.'

'Before I went to Milan—' Santino tensed, throwing her an anxious look '—I didn't know whether you were upset because you might be pregnant or upset because you might not be.'

'You should've told me up front that you didn't want a divorce any more,' Frankie censured.

'I needed you to make your own decision about what

you wanted…but I tried to show you in every way possible how much I cared…'

'I was afraid that was just because you thought I might be pregnant.'

'Now you know differently…' Santino curved his mouth with hungry fervour over hers and kissed her long and deeply until she shivered with need against him. 'But, having got so used to the idea that I was going to be a father, I was a little disappointed… But perhaps it was for the best. You're still only twenty-one. We've got plenty of time.'

'You'll be a father in time for Christmas,' Frankie confided breathlessly.

Santino was stunned. 'Say that again…'

Frankie explained the error of jumping to premature conclusions.

A slow smile of delighted satisfaction slashed Santino's darkly handsome features. 'So my reproductive cells won that battle on hostile territory…not so hostile after all, it seems.'

Frankie blushed as he drew her down on the bed with a strong look of intent in his lustrous dark eyes. 'I found the teddy in the limo,' she told him.

'We'll call her Flora…she can hen-peck Hamish. I was planning to gauge your mood with her and suggest that if you really wanted a baby we try again.'

'What would you have done if I *had* taken all that money?' Frankie asked reflectively.

'I would've concentrated on rehabilitating you. I couldn't possibly have let you go at the end of the three weeks. I love you too much, *piccola mia*.' Shrewdly assessing the faintly troubled look still tensing her face, Santino added, 'I can afford to look after your mother, but this time I'll ensure she is kept within reasonable bounds—'

'No…it wouldn't be right for you to support her again,' Frankie protested, strongly convinced that Della was young and able enough to support herself through her own efforts, and that any other arrangement would be akin to rewarding her for her dishonesty.

'Allow me to know what is right just this once,' Santino murmured, strongly amused by the steely glint in Frankie's gaze. 'I promise you that I will wreak the revenge of a lifetime when I see Della's reaction to the news that we are about to make her a grandmother!'

Since he chose that exact same moment to extract another feverishly hungry kiss, Frankie's ability to argue was severely diminished. Her quivering body strained up into the hard heat of his virile frame and she caught fire, driven by a primal need to seal their love in the most physical way possible.

'Hal is very fond of children,' Della confided rather unnecessarily as her third husband, a rock-solid middle-aged Texan rancher, cradled her grandchild with deft hands and made chortling sounds to amuse him. 'In fact...he would like us to try for one.'

At that unexpected news, Frankie's eyes opened very wide.

Her attractive mother reddened and gave her an uncertain glance. 'I know I was pretty hopeless with you, but Hal thinks that I'd cope much better now because I'd have his support and I'm more mature.'

Nothing came so readily to Della's lips these days as 'Hal thinks...' Hal Billings, burly, blunt-spoken and bossy, had rescued Della from her job on a department store beauty counter. While she was trying to sell him perfume Hal had fallen in love, and Della, who hadn't had the slightest intention of ever falling in love again, had fallen hardest of all.

Hal was comfortably off, but he considered idleness a vice and was fond of what he called 'plain living'. Della had had to make sacrifices to meet Hal's high standards, but she had done so with surprising eagerness.

Frankie had finally appreciated that her mother had been a deeply unhappy woman, who had tried to use material things to fill the emptiness inside her. Now a new love and a challenging lifestyle with a man she could rely on had given her the chance to make a fresh start.

Having reclaimed their son, Marco, Santino strode across the room with him, his lean, strong face concerned. 'I think Marco should bow out of his big day now...what do you think?'

Frankie stretched out her arms to receive her baby, gazing down at his sleepy little face, the dark silk fans of his lashes sinking over eyes as green as her own. 'Yes...he deserves some peace and quiet.'

But it still took another half-hour for them to work through the crush of their combined relatives and make an escape. Gino Caparelli and Alvaro Vitale were in close conversation in a corner. Frankie's great-aunts, initially as nervous as they were excited about leaving the village to come all the way to the *castello*, where Santino and Frankie had decided to hold the christening, were now happily chatting with two elderly ladies from Santino's side of the family.

'He is a little darling...a precious child,' Sonia Vitale sighed, her face softening as she delicately smoothed the soft black hair lying on her sleeping grandson's brow.

Frankie smiled. Her mother-in-law's unconcealed delight in her grandchild had done much to bring down the barriers between the two women. After a decade of living in near seclusion, nourishing her grief for the son she had lost, Sonia was returning to the business of living again.

With amusement, Santino was watching Della rush to fetch a cold drink for Hal. 'When you insisted that your mother give up the house and find a job, it was you I was worried about, *cara*. I thought she would never forgive you for being so tough, but you did her a favour. She's a changed woman.'

'She's even considering motherhood again,' Frankie confided.

After an arrested pause, Santino burst out laughing. 'There's method in her madness,' he pointed out. 'If she has a baby, Hal might let her off some of the chores round the ranch!'

Together, Santino and Frankie put their son down for a nap in his cosy crib. In perfect concert, they moved into each other's arms.

Frankie thought back on the first blissful year of their marriage. Matt had found another partner for the travel agency. She had had an easy pregnancy and Marco had been born with very little fuss. The joy of becoming parents had brought her and Santino even closer together. Santino adored his son. They spent quite a lot of weekends in Sardinia. Some day Marco was destined to hear about his family's humble beginnings on that hillside above La Rocca, just as Santino had learned his from his late grandfather.

'Have I made you happy?' Santino murmured huskily as they walked down the corridor.

Frankie gazed up into those lethally dark and sexy eyes and went weak at the knees, and gloried in the sensation. 'Head-over-heels happy. When I picked you out at sixteen, I knew what I was doing.'

'And I didn't know what had hit me,' Santino confided, dark head bending with the suggestion of a male yielding to an irresistible force. 'But I'm incredibly glad I was picked.' With that ragged confession, their lips met in hungry rediscovery, and it took the couple a suspiciously long time to make it back to the family celebration.

HARLEQUIN PRESENTS®

Everyone has special occasions in their life—an engagement, a wedding, an anniversary...or maybe the birth of a baby.

These are times of celebration and excitement, and we're delighted to bring you a special new series called...

One special occasion—that changes your life forever!

Celebrate *The Big Event!* with great books by some of your favorite authors:

September 1998—BRIDE FOR A YEAR
by Kathryn Ross (#1981)
October 1998—MARRIAGE MAKE UP
by Penny Jordan (#1983)
November 1998—RUNAWAY FIANCÉE
by Sally Wentworth (#1992)
December 1998—BABY INCLUDED!
by Mary Lyons (#1997)

Look in the back pages of any *Big Event* book to find out how to receive a set of sparkling wineglasses.

Available wherever Harlequin books are sold.

HARLEQUIN®
Makes any time special ™

Not The Same Old Story!

Exciting, glamorous romance stories that take readers around the world.

Sparkling, fresh and tender love stories that bring you pure romance.

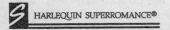

Bold and adventurous— Temptation is strong women, bad boys, great sex!

Provocative and realistic stories that celebrate life and love.

Contemporary fairy tales—where anything is possible and where dreams come true.

HARLEQUIN® INTRIGUE®

Heart-stopping, suspenseful adventures that combine the best of romance and mystery.

LOVE & LAUGHTER™

Humorous and romantic stories that capture the lighter side of love.

All work and no play?
Not these men!

July 1998
MACKENZIE'S LADY by Dallas Schulze

Undercover agent Mackenzie Donahue's
lazy smile and deep blue eyes were his best
weapons. But after rescuing—and kissing!—
damsel in distress Holly Reynolds, how could
he betray her by spying on her brother?

August 1998
MISS LIZ'S PASSION by Sherryl Woods

Todd Lewis could put up a building with ease,
but quailed at the sight of a classroom! Still,
Liz Gentry, his son's teacher, was no battle-ax,
and soon Todd started planning some
extracurricular activities of his own....

September 1998
A CLASSIC ENCOUNTER
by Emilie Richards

Doctor Chris Matthews was intelligent, sexy
and *very* good with his hands—which made
him all the more dangerous to single mom
Lizette St. Hilaire. So how long could she
resist Chris's special brand of TLC?

Available at your favorite retail outlet!

MEN AT WORK™

Look us up on-line at: http://www.romance.net   PMAW2